THE MARSHAL'S RUNAWAY WITNESS

DIANE BURKE

HARLEQUIN® LOVE INSPIRED® SUSPENSE

Recycling programs
for this product may
not exist in your area.

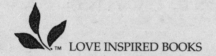

LOVE INSPIRED BOOKS

ISBN-13: 978-0-373-44700-8

The Marshal's Runaway Witness

Copyright © 2015 by Diane Burke

www.Harlequin.com

Printed in U.S.A.

"Do you have any idea who might want you dead?"

He chuckled, but there was no humor in his tone. "Let me rephrase that. Do you have any idea which one of the many people your father has hired to kill you may have actually tried to do it?"

She shook her head, and the sudden movement flashed pain through her head and made her nauseated.

"My father didn't put a contract out on me."

Dylan stared at her, disbelief written all over his face.

"He wouldn't," she insisted. "If I had remained with you and testified against him, then he would have felt he had no choice. I understand that. But when I left witness protection and disappeared, he knew I was no longer a threat."

"After everything that has happened, do you really believe that?"

"Yes, I do. But don't you see? You've changed all that. If he finds out that I am in your custody again, he will believe I have accepted witness protection. Now I will be a danger to him. Now he probably will put out a contract on me. You have to let me go. You have to let me get out of here."

"That's not happening." They locked gazes. "We are still getting you to that trial and putting you on the stand."

Diane Burke is an award-winning author who has had six books published with Love Inspired Suspense. She is a voracious reader and loves movies, crime shows, travel and eating out! She has never met a stranger, only people she hasn't had the pleasure of talking to yet. She loves to hear from readers and can be reached at diane@dianeburkeauthor.com. She can also be found on Twitter and Facebook.

Books by Diane Burke

Love Inspired Suspense

Midnight Caller
Double Identity
Bounty Hunter Guardian
Silent Witness
Hidden in Plain View
The Marshal's Runaway Witness

May you be able to feel and understand, as all God's children should, how long, how wide, how deep, and how high His love really is; and to experience this love for yourselves, though it is so great that you will never see the end of it or fully know or understand it.
–Ephesians 3:18-19

Thank you with all my heart
to the Volusia County Romance Writers group for helping
me brainstorm this story. They were great at helping me
fill in the Swiss cheese holes in my plot. You're a great
group of writers and I don't know what I'd do without you!

I also wish to thank Nancy Orlandi,
who suffered through every revision, every author doubt,
and came up with some pretty good ideas
when I needed them. I appreciate it more than you know.

ONE

Unease crept up Angelina Baroni's spine. The kind of unease a person feels when she thinks she's being watched but doesn't see anyone.

The tinkling of laughter and the sound of distant voices drifting on the Atlantic City ocean breeze couldn't pull her out of her funk. Not even the incessant chattering and giggles of her best friend and business partner, Maria Lopez, could calm her dark mood as they strolled the beach.

Something was wrong.

She couldn't put her finger on it but her senses flashed warning signs. She wouldn't be alive today if she hadn't paid attention to those inner warnings over the past three years. It unsettled her to have them crop up again.

Nothing unusual had happened during their marketing meeting tonight. On the contrary, Maria had given an excellent presentation. They'd signed a lucrative advertising contract with one of the larger casinos. This was a huge milestone for their tiny firm. First time they'd gone up against the corporate advertising giants and won.

They'd celebrated with dinner in the swanky dining room they would now promote and were walking off the huge calorie overload at the edge of the surf. Maria had worked hard for this account. Her enthusiasm was contagious and Angelina couldn't be happier for her, for them.

Still.

A sense of foreboding crawled up her body like a bug she'd been unable to swipe away.

She glanced over her shoulder.

Nothing.

No one.

But someone was there. In the darkness. Watching them. Waiting. She could *feel* it.

The pale glow from a full moon provided extra illumination. Except for the two of them, the beach was deserted. She glanced at the boardwalk. People walked back and forth in a continuous motion. No one stopped to stare at them over the rails.

Her gaze settled on the area under the pier. Had she seen someone move in the shadows or was her mind playing tricks on her? She stared harder into the darkness. Nothing.

But that feeling of being watched...

Her stomach clenched.

She trusted her gut. This familiar, although unwanted, tightness told her she was missing something.

But what?

A splash of cold water hit her face.

"Hey, Angie! You haven't heard a word I've said."

It took her a second to respond to the shortened name. Believing her life was in jeopardy, she'd run away from the witness protection program, trusting no one but herself to keep her alive. She'd changed her name, staying close to her birth name so she'd respond to it easily, yet even three years later she still occasionally hesitated. Now Angelina Baroni, aka Angie Robertson, wiped the salt water from her cheek and grinned at Maria. "I've been listening. And stop throwing water at me. It's cold."

"It's October, silly. The ocean is supposed to be cold. Don't change the subject. You've been ignoring me." Maria's short black hair with its one large aqua streak blew in the wind. Strands danced across her freckled nose and coiled in her large hoop earrings.

"I heard every word."

"Okay, fine. Tell me what theme I'm going to use for our first ad?"

Busted! She'd tried to listen. Honestly, she had. But that unsettled feeling had distracted her.

"See! I was right. You weren't listening." Maria stooped and splashed her again.

Angelina threw her hands up to protect herself and laughed. "Enough!"

"Our first casino! Can you believe it?" Throwing her arms wide and her face to the heavens, Maria spun around. On one of her passes she threw a glance Angie's way and stopped in midtwirl.

"Okay. What gives? Something's bothering you." Maria shot a look in each direction. "What?" Her expression sobered. "Ang? You look scared to death. What is it? What's wrong?"

"Nothing. I'm being paranoid." She stared into the darkness under the pier again. "It's just..." She didn't see anyone, no moving shadows this time, only darkness. "Forget it. I'm being silly." She turned her attention back to her friend and grinned. "I'm so proud of you. You did a great job tonight."

"Thanks." Marie grinned in return. "Just think, Ang. We've worked so hard. Now all our dreams are about to come true!"

Something whizzed past Angelina's ear.

Before her mind could identify the sound, another bullet whizzed past. This one landed in a soft thud.

A small patch of moisture formed on the left side of Maria's dress.

Angelina blinked in shock and stared at the stain. Blood?

Oh dear, it is *blood!*

A surprised expression appeared on Maria's face moments before her body began to crumble.

Angelina rushed forward. Bullets kicked up the sand where she'd been standing only moments before.

"Maria!" She caught her friend in her arms. "No!"

Tears burned her eyes. Her arms begged to release the heavy weight but she couldn't. Not yet. She clasped her friend against her body. Her arms ached with the strain of the deadweight. Her heart breaking with the sorrow.

Dear Lord, be with Maria. Carry her home in Your arms.

Slowly, gently, she lowered her friend to the sand.

The prayer had been automatic, instinctive. Angelina had stopped praying years before to God, whom she believed never answered her prayers. But she couldn't take the prayer back. Not this time.

Two more bullets hit the water, each one closer than the last.

Springing into action, Angelina zigzagged across

the beach, doing everything she could not to be an easy target. If she could reach the boardwalk she'd be safe. Lights, people, help loomed only a few dozen yards ahead.

Almost there.

She pushed harder, her feet fighting her as they sank into the soft sand. Her calves cramped beneath the punishing pace. Her breath bubbled in short gasps, each one feeling like her last.

Only a few more yards.

She never heard the bullet that claimed her. Never felt the pain as the velocity of the shot threw her to the ground.

I've been hit.

That was her last conscious thought as a second bullet sent her into blessed oblivion.

US marshal Dylan McKnight stormed down the hospital corridor and came to an abrupt halt outside one of the rooms. US marshal Thomas "Bear" Simmons stood with his back against the closed door.

Dylan never knew whether the man had gotten his nickname from his enormous linebacker girth or the fact that his huge hands could be mistaken for lethal weapons. Either way he never thought of his partner as anything less than the bear of a man he was.

"Is it true?" At six foot one Dylan still had to look up at the gentle giant.

Bear held his hands up and grinned. "Hey man, I know better than to play with you about this. Yeah, it's true. Angelina Baroni is inside."

Dylan exhaled slowly. He'd thought about what he'd

do if he ever saw her again. Prayed about it. Now the time was here and he didn't feel he could move a muscle.

His mind's eye immediately captured the memory of long thick black hair framing a heart-shaped face. Twinkling sky-blue eyes. Natural blush-tinged cheeks. Lips, touched lightly with red, smiling back so mysteriously, she could give the *Mona Lisa* a run for its money.

His Angelina.

His nightmare was more like it.

He'd had one job to do. Keep his witness alive and hidden in protective custody until the upcoming trial of Vincenzo Baroni, New Jersey capo. Head of one of the strongest arms of organized crime to hit this area since the olden days of Capone and Luciano.

Ruthless.

Elusive.

Untouchable.

He had had Vincenzo dead to rights. His own daughter Angelina was going to testify against him. But Dylan had broken a cardinal rule—never get involved with a witness.

He'd trusted Angelina, after all he'd known her since grammar school, but he should have known better. He'd been burned once before by trusting a witness. The bad information had led to a shoot-out that killed his partner and had almost cost him his life, as well. He couldn't believe he'd allowed his tendency to trust to burn them again.

Angelina had proven without doubt that she was her father's daughter. She'd played him. Made a fool out of him. Disappeared without a trace. Almost ruined his career. Definitely ruined his case.

Thankfully, there had still been enough circumstantial evidence for the grand jury to indict. Now, after three long years and multiple attempts of the defense attorneys to delay, the case was finally going to trial.

With his star witness missing and the trial starting in six days, he'd been unable to sleep, eat or do anything else these past few weeks but pray.

God had cut it close answering those prayers. But He'd answered. Angelina was on the other side of that door.

His heart thundered against his chest. He shot a glance at Bear. "What happened? How is she?"

Dylan wanted to push past his partner into the room and find out for himself but he steeled himself to remain professional and in control. Something he should have done three years ago and hadn't. He'd put his heart on the line and he'd been burned.

"She took a couple of bullets. One in the right arm. One grazed her head."

His stomach clenched as if he'd been sucker punched. No matter what had happened between them he couldn't bear the thought of anyone hurting her.

"She probably has a concussion. We're waiting for the doctor to brief us." Bear stepped away from the door. "She's one blessed lady. The woman with her was brought in dead on arrival."

Again, Dylan winced, offered a prayer of gratitude that Angelina hadn't died and offered a brief prayer for the woman who had.

"Did they nab the shooter?" Dylan placed his hand on the door but paused for the answer.

Bear shook his head. "So far no witnesses. We have our suspicions but you know how that goes."

Dylan nodded and pushed open the door.

The room, illuminated only by the night-light over the bed, revealed a small female form lying beneath the blankets.

Dylan stepped closer.

Short errant strands of hair peeked from beneath the gauze bandage across her head.

Red hair?

Who would have thought?

A smile touched his lips. Cute, though.

Almost as if it had a mind of its own, his hand brushed a wisp from her forehead.

He'd forgiven her years ago as God asks everyone to do. Forgiveness was the easy part.

It was forgetting he was having trouble with.

She stirred beneath his touch.

His hand froze. The warmth of her smooth, velvety skin seared his skin. His pulse skipped a beat. His eyes strayed to her slightly parted lips. She'd been his best friend in grammar school and their relationship had become full of teenage angst in middle school. Gazing at her now stirred those memories.

He took a deep breath, stared at the sleeping woman for another minute, and then lowered his hand to his side.

Once upon a time he'd believed he was falling in love with her. Until...

A slow, steady burn rose from his gut and he allowed the anger to flow like molten lava through his veins.

Anger would help him remain professional and keep his personal feelings at bay. Anger would keep him sharp and focused. Anger would prevent him from falling for her lies or betrayals ever again.

TWO

Pain.

Deep, throbbing pain.

Angelina raised a hand to her forehead. A thick gauze bandage made her pause.

What?

She opened her eyes. A lightning bolt of hurt shot through her head and she squeezed them closed again.

Okay. Stay still and think. Where are you? What happened?

It didn't take long for her mental fog to lift. Everything came rushing back and she wished it hadn't. The shooting. Her best friend, Maria, dead.

She shot up in bed and instantly regretted it. The room spun like an amusement park ride out of control. Her stomach turned over. She held her head with both hands and groaned aloud.

"Good. You're awake."

Angelina froze like a person who had stumbled upon a deadly rattler. She'd recognize that voice anywhere.

Dylan McKnight.

How had he found her? The last time she had seen

US deputy marshal Dylan McKnight he was conspiring to have her killed.

She hadn't wanted to believe it. Wouldn't have believed it if she hadn't witnessed it with her own eyes.

Angelina had been sitting in a holding room waiting to testify before the grand jury. She knew her testimony would go a long way in helping them determine whether there was enough evidence to indict her father for murder.

Nerves had skittered up her spine. Her legs had bounced up and down and her hands wouldn't stop shaking. Unable to sit still another second, she sprang up from her chair and paced the room. On one of her passes she glanced out the door into the hall and saw Dylan slip the bailiff a piece of paper. Minutes later the bailiff, who had a sinister look in his eyes and a sneer on his lips, passed that note to her.

Do you really think you will live to testify? I own cops. I own judges. I own the marshals that pretend to protect you. You will never be able to hide from me.

The note had broken her heart. If she hadn't seen the exchange she would not have believed it. During the few short months they were together in the witness protection program before she fled, she'd started to have feelings for Dylan and had believed they were returned.

How could she have been so wrong?

She'd tried to give him the benefit of the doubt. Maybe Dylan had given the bailiff a different note. Or maybe Dylan hadn't read the note and was just a go-between passing it from an outside source to the bailiff.

Maybe.

But could she trust her own judgment anymore? She'd trusted her father, believed him when he claimed to be a successful businessman who was the brunt of vicious rumors by envious competitors. She'd believed Dylan when he told her he cared about her and promised to keep her safe.

She'd been wrong about both the men closest to her.

Her father had turned out to be a cold-blooded murderer.

And Dylan...

Even if Dylan hadn't known the contents of the note, he'd still let the bailiff come close enough to give it to her, close enough to kill her if he had wanted. She couldn't trust Dylan to keep her safe. The note proved she couldn't trust the marshals, the cops, even the bailiff! A heavy lead weight had formed in the pit of her stomach and with sickening clarity she'd known the truth. She couldn't trust *anyone* anymore except herself—not even God.

And for the past three years that was exactly what she'd done—protected herself.

Until last night...

Dylan approached the head of the hospital bed. "What's the matter, Angelina? Have nothing to say to an old friend?"

The warmth of the US marshal's breath fanned her cheek when he spoke. She couldn't be sure whether it was his words causing her pulse to trip or if it was the proximity of the man himself, the man who long ago had made her pulse race for reasons that had nothing to do with fear.

Did he have to stand so close?

There was a time when she would have welcomed his nearness.

But that was a lifetime ago. Three years had changed her. Three years had changed everything.

"Did you really think you could pull it off?" Dylan crossed his arms like an angry sentinel blocking all means of escape.

One glance into his dark, penetrating, *hostile* eyes brought her back to her senses. Her nerve endings danced in fear. What was he going to do with her now? She had betrayed him—and the years had not erased the memory.

She needed to run again—now, this minute—as far and as fast as she could. If she could only stop the shooting pain in her head and clear her blurred vision.

"Please…"

Please what? Even she didn't know what she was trying to say. Where did that empty plea come from? Did she really think he could forget what she'd done?

A sense of dread cloaked her body like a heavy blanket. She inhaled deeply, exhaled slowly, trying not to panic. Somehow she needed to buy time while she tried to figure out her next move. She didn't know what to do. She didn't even know where she was. Her gaze skittered about the room.

Okay. She was in a hospital.

A tightness drew her attention to the bandage squeezing her right arm. An IV was connected to her left hand and a steel rail guarded the left side of her bed.

A dull throb claimed the space right between her eyes. Sluggish, unfocused thoughts made her head spin as if she was trying to resurface from deep waters.

The pounding in her head became a full-fledged gallop of pain as the significance of the night's events slammed into her. Every cell in her body screamed.

You're in danger. Get out of here. Run!

She threw the covers off and tried to swing her legs from the bed.

Her head swam and her eyes refused to focus.

"Where do you think you're going? You are in no shape to be getting out of bed."

She ignored Dylan's words and tried a second time to stand. When her feet hit the floor, her legs, shaking as if they didn't have a bone in them, stubbornly refused to hold her weight.

Two familiar, strong hands clasped her waist, supporting her, keeping her from hitting the cold linoleum in the white-washed room. Angelina knew she shouldn't but she welcomed the strength of his sturdy male torso and leaned heavily against him.

The sound of his heartbeat beneath her ear soothed her. The warmth of his body made her want to burrow deeper in his arms. The woodsy aroma of his cologne mingling with his own masculine scent brought a smile to her lips and stirred pleasant memories.

Seeking reassurance she lifted her head, gazed into his dark brown eyes, and found none. Only questions, hurt and disappointment stared back. His coldness and anger unnerved her.

He couldn't be on her father's payroll. Could he? Either way, she knew she wasn't safe in his care.

Dylan gently lowered her onto the bed. He pulled the blanket over her. The clipped tone in his voice vibrated with controlled anger but it was the gentleness of his hands as he tucked her blankets in and adjusted her pillow that offered her safety, comfort and hope.

"What can you tell me about what happened last night?"

Angelina lowered her head and remained silent.

"Don't you remember?"

"Maria and I were taking a walk when…when…"

When she couldn't find any more words, Dylan filled in the blanks.

"The police report states the two of you were walking last night down by the pier. Shots rang out. You ran for safety. You made it. Your friend didn't."

The brutal honesty of his words stung her.

She squirmed beneath his scrutiny but remained silent.

"Do you remember now?"

How much should she tell him? What should she say? If he was working for her father, was he trying to find out if she could identify her shooter? Or was he simply a US marshal trying to do his job? Either way, she knew she needed to choose her words carefully.

"I'm sorry. I can't help you…" Her voice trailed off.

"Did you see the person who shot you?" Dylan waited for her answer.

She grimaced and touched the bandage on her forehead again. "I was shot?"

"Are you in pain?" A softer tone laced his words. "Do you want me to summon a nurse?"

"No."

The hallway door opened. The figure of a large man, his silhouette outlined by the outside hall light, appeared in the doorway, his face in shadows.

A wave of panic stole Angelina's breath. Dylan wasn't the only one who had found her.

The killer found me. I'm no longer safe.

"Run!" She threw her body over the railing on the opposite side of the bed and promptly splatted like a pancake on the floor. Even her teeth vibrated with pain.

Dylan hurried around the bed. "Are you crazy? What are you trying to do?" He ran his hands lightly over her limbs, checking for broken bones. "That concussion must have scrambled your brains. Don't move. Are you hurt?"

She had pulled the IV out of her hand during the fall. Almost in a daze she held it up in front of her face and stared at the blood trickling down her skin.

"Now look at what you've done." Dylan pressed a clean, white handkerchief to the back of her hand to stanch the bleeding. "What were you thinking by pulling a stunt like that?"

The man in the doorway threw on the overhead light and hurried forward. "Is she okay? Should I get a nurse?"

"She's fine." Dylan scooped her up in his arms as though she weighed nothing more than a feather and deposited her back in the bed.

Angelina guarded her eyes against the bright fluorescent light that had replaced the soft glow of the night-light above her bed. Shadows no longer hid this second man's face. US marshal Robert "Bear" Simmons, Dylan's partner and the other half of the team she'd duped, had entered the room.

"Good to see you again, Ms. Baroni." Dylan's partner grinned widely showing a mouthful of even white teeth against coffee-brown skin. "Imagine my surprise to find that you've been hiding right under our noses."

Her eyes shot to Dylan.

For what? Reassurance? Safety? Help?

Dylan flashed that devastatingly handsome smile she had once found so hard to resist, that same smile that could draw her to him again if she wasn't careful, but it lacked the warmth it used to hold.

She glanced away. She couldn't afford to be careless again. Her life depended on it.

"I'll ask you again..." She could feel Dylan's eyes boring into her as he spoke. "Can you identify your shooter?"

"No. I didn't see a thing. I was too busy running for my life."

"Do you have any idea who might want you dead?" He chuckled but there was no humor in his tone. "Let me rephrase that. Do you have any idea which one of the many people your father has hired to kill you may have actually tried to do it?"

She shook her head and the sudden movement flashed pain through her head and made her nauseous.

"My father didn't put a contract out on me."

Dylan stared at her, disbelief written all over his face.

"He wouldn't," she insisted. "If I'd remained with you and testified against him, then he would have felt he had no choice. I understand that. But when I left witness protection and disappeared, he knew I was no longer a threat."

"After everything that has happened, do you really believe that?"

"Yes, I do. But don't you see, you've changed all that. If he finds out that I'm in your custody again, he'll believe I've accepted witness protection. Now I will be a danger to him. Now he probably will put out a contract on me. You have to let me go. You have to let me get out of here."

"That's not happening." They locked gazes. "Whether you testify voluntarily or whether the district attorney will have to call you as a hostile witness, we are still getting you to that trial and putting you on the stand."

Angelina slid farther down her bed. She wished she could pull the blanket over her head and just make the world disappear. She'd been so careful. But in seconds her world had crashed around her and she didn't have a clue how to make things right.

"I… I've already told you that I didn't see anyone. I was walking with my friend Maria on the beach and then…"

Silence loomed between them.

"Please…" she whispered. "I need to rest. Please leave. I really can't help you."

"Leave?" Dylan's mirthless laugh echoed loudly in the room. "Not a chance. I made the mistake of leaving you alone once before. Remember?" He moved closer so that only she could hear his words. "You lied to me." His eyes darkened. "You walked into the bathroom, climbed out the window and took off. Made a fool out of me. Damaged my credibility with my boss." He squared his shoulders and took a step back.

His voice hardened. "Did you really think I would forget? I haven't forgotten anything."

Heat burned her cheeks with shame and regret over their last night together, over the way she'd lead him on to think they were going to have their first romantic evening but had deceived him instead and ran away.

A variety of emotions flashed across Dylan's face. He was as upset by this meeting as she was.

But how could that be? He was acting like the injured party. Is it possible she'd been wrong about her suspicions?

A twinge of conscience made her feel guilty. She hadn't wanted to hurt anybody, especially not him. But even if she'd misread the note situation, she hadn't been wrong about him letting the bailiff within arm's reach of her. She had to keep reminding herself of the facts. US marshal or not, Dylan couldn't keep his promise. He couldn't be trusted to keep her safe. She'd had no choice but to run. And, if she wanted to live, soon she would have to find a way to run again.

Dylan appeared to recover quickly, the raw emotions that flitted over his face were gone and his features hardened like carved granite. But when he spoke his words were gentle. "I'm sorry about Maria."

The tears Angelina had been fighting so hard to hold back flowed freely down her cheeks.

She remembered the shocked, empty look in Maria's eyes, the weight of her body as she'd lowered her friend to the sand. She couldn't imagine a day, didn't want to imagine a day, without Maria in her life.

"Thank you." Her words came out a whisper.

"Over the years, I've struggled with the possibility you might be dead. When you disappeared that night, I thought somehow your father's organization had kidnapped you. It took me a while to understand that you fled on your own."

Was that pain she heard in his voice? Could it be?

"I find it hard to believe you hid in plain sight for three years and didn't run into the deadly end of a bullet before now." Dylan's voice softened. "I'm grateful you're still alive."

Angelina studied his expression. He seemed sincere. How could she know for sure? She had no faith in her ability to judge a person's character anymore. If he were going to harm her, wouldn't he have done it by now? Maybe Dylan had never been on her father's payroll. Maybe she'd been wrong. Or maybe not. How could she know whether she could trust this man with her life or not?

If Dylan didn't know better, he would think Angelina was afraid of him. He chided himself. Didn't he know by now that she had that sweet, vulnerable act down to a science? He'd fallen for it once. He wouldn't fall for it again.

He couldn't believe she'd been able to survive on her own all this time. He'd carried a heavy burden of guilt for not being able to keep her safe every day since she'd disappeared. He'd been certain that one day he'd come across her dead body and he often wondered how he would ever face it if he did.

But she wasn't dead.

She was alive and, although injured and hurting, he was certain she was warily looking for an escape route. He couldn't let his guard down for a second.

The panic shining in her eyes reminded him of a helplessly injured and frightened animal. His conscience made him regret that he had to treat her so callously. But the memory of her setup and her betrayal was all it took to keep him on guard.

"Who knows I'm here?" She clasped his hand.

He felt the trembling in her fingers. The panic in her eyes made her appear vulnerable and terrified. She seemed barely able to hold it together and for a moment he felt sorry for her.

But only for a moment. He knew what she was capable of, after all she was her father's daughter, and he would do well to remember it.

"I have to get out of here, Dylan. I'm not safe." Her eyes pleaded with him.

"Don't worry. I'm not going to let anything happen to you. There are only a handful of people who know who you are—or where you are—and they are on a need-to-know basis."

The flash of doubt on her face surprised him.

He pulled his hand away from hers. "Get some sleep. You need your rest."

"You don't understand. If anyone other than you and Bear knows that I am here, then my safety is already in jeopardy."

Dylan glanced over his shoulder at Bear. "Did you get the protection unit set up outside the room?"

"Yep, 24/7. Detective Donahue loaned us some of his men. No one will be allowed into this room without furnishing proper identification."

Angelina laughed mirthlessly. "You think a cop sitting outside my door is going to protect me? You think my father isn't capable of corrupting a nurse or a doctor with stellar credentials to gain access to this room?" She flailed her arms. "How about the janitor mopping the floors and emptying the waste bins? It isn't a matter of *if* my father can infiltrate this joke of protection you're offering me, it's when."

She pushed hard against Dylan's chest. "Move out of my way. I have to get out of here now!"

"Shhh!" Dylan pulled her to him, his arms steel bands holding her against his chest. "You're safe, Angelina. I'm not going to let anything happen to you. Trust me."

It took her a few minutes to stop struggling and calm down. When she did, she raised her head from his chest. Her eyes challenged him. "Why should I trust you?"

A bittersweet smile twisted his lips. "Because I didn't betray you. You are the one who betrayed me."

THREE

Dylan's words settled over the room like a dark thundercloud. An ominous silence ensued between them.

Bear shook his head and emitted a low whistle. "Things are getting a little too dicey in here for me. You two work this out. I'll be outside the door making sure everything's set."

After Bear stepped outside, Angelina sat on the edge of the bed. She looked into Dylan's eyes and tried to find answers to her unasked questions. She sighed. She didn't trust him. She didn't believe he could keep her safe but she realized, for right now, there wasn't a thing she could do about it.

"What do you have planned?" She grimaced and again fingered the bandage wrapped across her forehead as a lightning bolt of pain grabbed her. "How long do I have to stay here?"

"Not long. I've already put things in motion to have a safe house ready as soon as you're discharged."

"And if I don't want to go to a safe house? If I don't want to cooperate?"

Dylan didn't respond. The hard glint in his eyes did the talking for him.

Once there had been warmth and gentleness in Dylan's demeanor. Though she understood his coldness and distance, it still surprised her and she wished for just a flash of that former warmth.

"Are you certain it was my father who killed Maria and shot me?"

"I doubt whether your father was the actual shooter. He's too smart to dirty his hands a second time. But did he order the hit? What do you think? You are the only person standing between him and a date with a lethal injection."

"Sometimes it's hard for me to believe my father is trying to have me killed." She shrugged. "He's my dad. What kind of dad tries to kill his own daughter?" She didn't know what hurt more, the physical pain of her injuries or the emotional pain of trying to deal with the current situation. "When I left protective custody, I thought Dad would believe I'd changed my mind about testifying and would no longer pose a threat. It's why I felt safer staying in this area." Her shoulders sagged beneath the weight of the truth. "I was wrong." She gazed up at him. "Maybe about a lot of things."

"Why, Angelina?"

She knew his question wasn't about her father or her decision to remain in Atlantic City. She saw all of the pain, confusion and anger in his eyes. His question was about them.

Three years ago their relationship had been new and exciting. Their time together in protective custody cemented the friendship they'd shared as kids and laid the foundation for something more meaningful as adults. They spent nights talking in front of the fire about shared interests and goals. Their many walks on the grounds of their hideaway led them to discover a mutual love of nature. Angelina believed there might be a possibility of a future together. Until the note exchange made her lose her faith in him.

Dylan wore his emotions on his face and she knew this reunion wasn't easy on either one of them. She could see how he struggled. Part of him tried to put on a professional air and act as though the past hadn't happened.

But the other part of him…

When he looked at her, she saw his pain. Yet the anger in his face was tempered by the gentleness of his touch. She knew he wondered if what they'd shared had been real or merely a ploy. She wondered the same thing of him.

But none of it mattered now. She couldn't give him answers she didn't have. It had been another time and place. A moment of stability in a world of chaos. A safe haven.

But real?

The only thing *real* anymore was that Dylan McKnight was law enforcement and that meant he couldn't be trusted.

Angelina rubbed her face with her hands. "I need to get out of here. I need to get away…" Her voice trailed off.

"Angelina, you saw your father murder your neighbor, a man you knew very well. I don't care if he's your father or not. I can't believe you're hesitating about testifying after what you saw him do."

When she spoke her words were merely a whisper. "You don't understand."

"Explain it to me."

Her eyes challenged him. "I hated what he did. It made me sick. It made me scared. Of course, I wanted him punished. I still do."

"Then why did you run?"

Wetness welled in her eyes.

"I wanted to live! I didn't believe you or anyone else could keep me safe. It was stupid…and selfish…and… and…" Agony sliced through her body. "Because I only cared about myself, my best friend, the funniest, most wonderful individual I have ever known, is dead." Her voice cracked on a sob.

"Maria's death is not your fault." Dylan fisted his hands at his sides almost as if he had to fight to stay where he was and not come closer or offer her comfort.

She swiped a hand at the tears streaming down her cheeks. "Isn't it? If I hadn't been such a coward, if I'd stayed and testified against my father, Maria would be alive today. How is that not my fault?"

"I'm sorry you lost your friend. But you can't blame yourself."

"It tears me up inside to know my father is guilty of murder, that all the things said about him being a crime boss are true. He sheltered me from the truth my entire life. He acted just like everybody else's dad. He kept that part of his life totally hidden from me. I honestly didn't know. I didn't."

Dylan nodded his understanding but didn't interrupt.

"Do you have any idea how difficult and painful it is for me to know my father probably has a hit out on me right now. My father! The man I've trusted and loved my entire life has hired someone to kill me!"

If I can't trust my father, who took care of me after my mother died, how can I ever trust any other man?

No matter how much I may want to, how can I ever trust you?

She clasped her forehead in her hands almost as if she could hide her thoughts from him.

"I hate what he's done!" She spat out the words. "So many nights I prayed for God to bring him to justice." She balled the sheet in her fist. "But God didn't answer my prayers."

Bitterness spilled over in her words.

"I grew up believing God is a forgiving God. I don't want God to forgive this time, Dylan. I want vengeance."

Dylan's shocked expression gave her pause. "God insists we forgive others and leave judgment to Him. Pray. He'll help you through this."

"God has no place in my life anymore. I stopped believing in Him and the idea of forgiveness years ago."

"Don't give up on God, Angelina. He hasn't given up on you."

If only she could believe it. She changed the subject.

"When do I have to testify?"

"Monday. Less than a week away."

A week. She doubted she'd still be alive in a week.

"After you testify, the running will be over. You'll have your life back. You'll be free, never having to look over your shoulder or be afraid anymore."

"You can't keep me safe!" Raising her voice sent pain shooting through her head. Instantly she stopped talking.

He gently clasped her hand. "I'll protect you with my life, Angelina. Trust me."

Trust him? The note. The bailiff. How could she possibly trust him?

"How many lives are going to be lost before this is over, Dylan? Cops? Federal marshals? You? It's hard enough for me to live with the deaths I already know about. First, our neighbor. Then, Maria. If I survive this mess and others don't, how do you think I can live with the knowledge that other people lost their lives while trying to protect me?"

"Your father is a powerful man, Angelina. But he isn't God. I'm putting this in God's hands. He has brought down the mighty before."

"I'm going to testify," she assured him. "It's what I should have done years ago. If I had done it then when I should have, Maria wouldn't be dead. I just hope I can testify before anyone else dies."

"Don't worry about other people dying. We're all trained law enforcement officers. We're good at our jobs. We know how to protect ourselves and we can protect you." He crossed the room to the door. "I'm going to check with your doctor and see how soon we can move you."

"The sooner the better, Dylan. Every second I'm in this hospital room I am in danger and so is everyone else."

"Bear is right outside the door. I'll be back as soon as I confirm a few things."

She nodded.

As he turned to go she called his name and he glanced back over his shoulder.

"I'm sorry, Dylan. I didn't mean to… I didn't want to hurt you." She ended in little more than a whisper. "There were things about that night you don't know."

Dylan straightened his spine and held up his palm

to stop her almost as if he just couldn't handle this conversation right now.

"We'll talk about it later. My job right now is to get you out of here and keep you safe."

Without another word, he turned and strode out of the room.

Dr. Thompson looked up from reading the medical file displayed on the computer terminal when Dylan approached.

"Doctor, how soon can we safely move the patient in room 210?"

"I'd like to keep her at least tonight for observation. We removed the bullet in her arm but the one that grazed her skull could be more serious. Another fraction of an inch and we'd be talking a totally different outcome."

"Doc, if I don't get her out of here soon, tonight if possible," Dylan insisted, "I'm afraid her good fortune might run out. Tell me what I need to know to be able to take care of her yet still leave."

"She probably has a mild concussion. Keep her awake and alert as much as possible. When she does doze off, wake her up often and make her speak to you.

"She might suffer from blurred vision. Probably nausea. And I am certain she'll have pain." The doctor stepped over to one of the medication carts. He withdrew a card filled with pills from the cart and signed a chart before turning toward Dylan. "This will help with the nausea." He handed him the card. "But I am against giving you prescription-strength pain medication if she isn't here to be monitored."

"I understand. Isn't there something milder than narcotics that will at least keep the edge off her pain? I'd like to keep her as comfortable as possible."

The doctor paused a moment and then handed him a different card. "This should help but please monitor her carefully."

"I will. So what do you say? Can I get her out of here?"

"Yes. But call me if you run into problems. Better yet, if something goes wrong bring her back to the ER and page me immediately."

"Thanks, Doc. I appreciate it."

Dylan stepped away from the nurses station. He took out his cell, punched a number and wasn't surprised when his boss answered on the first ring.

"Well? Has she agreed to testify?" he asked without hesitation.

"Yes. But she's scared and I can't say I blame her. She's been on the run for over three years. Her best friend was killed. She was shot. She doesn't trust anyone right now. But she'll be all right by the time the trial begins next week."

"Good. Everything's almost set on our end. I'll text you the address of the safe house as soon as it's confirmed. Detective Donahue has arranged for some of his men and a few state troopers to escort you. They'll meet you on the lower level of the hospital by one of the back loading docks."

"Don't think that's a good idea, boss. I don't need a parade of cop cars drawing unnecessary attention to us. Bear and I can handle it."

"Like you handled it last time?"

An uncomfortable silence stretched across the airwaves.

"Okay," his boss relented. "We'll do it your way. No troopers. No cops. I sent Marshal Selma Washington to go with you. I don't want Angelina Baroni out of your sight. Having a female agent who can go everywhere Miss Baroni goes will guarantee we won't lose this witness a second time."

"I understand, sir." Dylan gritted his teeth but refrained from rebuttal. He deserved the dressing-down.

"Washington is probably already at the hospital," his boss continued. "I gave her the assignment hours ago and asked her to meet you in Baroni's room."

"Fine. I'm headed back there now."

"Call in when you get to the safe house."

"Will do."

"And, Dylan…"

"Sir?"

"I don't need to tell you how important it is to get Ms. Baroni to testify. The FBI are down my neck on this one. Along with ATF and even Homeland Security. Vincenzo Baroni has broken every federal law known to man and everybody wants in on the action. This woman has the power to bring down one of the strongest organized crime families we have seen in decades. Keep her alive and don't let her give you the slip again."

"Believe me, sir, no one wants that more than me." Dylan hung up and slid the phone back in his suit pocket. Angelina's betrayal had done much more than ding his male pride. It had put an indelible black mark on his career and he wasn't about to let her do it again. He'd bring her in to testify if he had to handcuff her to his left wrist and stay awake 24/7.

A sound, a specific sound not easily mistaken for anything else, drew his attention.

Couldn't be.
He froze, cocked his head to the side, and listened.
There it was again.
Pop! Pop!
Gunfire!

FOUR

Adrenaline surged through Dylan McKnight's body. He withdrew his weapon and pointed it toward the ceiling. His legs pounded the linoleum faster than he'd thought possible as he bolted toward Angelina's room.

"Move!" He skirted a patient on a walker. "Get out of my way!" He dodged a nurse pushing a wheelchair.

In the distance, he saw a familiar figure racing toward him.

Bear!

A woman, probably the other marshal, matched Bear's pace stride for stride as they sprinted forward. Angelina's petite figure was huddled between them as they half dragged, half carried her along.

"Get back in your rooms," Dylan shouted to hospital patients as he tried to close the distance between himself and his partner. "Get out of the corridor, now!"

Chaos ensued. People screamed and hospital personnel scurried to help the patients do as Dylan demanded.

Two men appeared at the end of the far corridor and were quickly gaining ground.

A shot rang out.

Bear, never losing stride, glanced over his shoulder, raised his right hand and fired his weapon.

A second shot rang out and a chunk of drywall chipped off next to Dylan's ear. He ducked and returned fire, offering what little cover he could for his partner.

One of the men in pursuit fell to the ground.

The second man stopped, grabbed his injured accomplice under the arm, and dragged him to his feet. In a hail of bullets, they ducked down another hall.

Dylan returned fire again, then again.

When they disappeared from sight, he stopped firing and tried to make a split-second decision on what his next move should be. He wanted to pursue them but there were three people at hand that needed him more. If there were two bad guys, it stood to reason there would soon be more. His priority right now was getting his team to safety.

"I'll take over. Thanks." Dylan nudged Selma away. He slipped his hand under Angelina's left arm but not before passing Selma his car keys and telling her where their black sedan was parked. "Bring the car back to the loading dock. We'll be right behind you. Go!"

No longer burdened with Angelina's weight, Selma didn't need any prodding and took off running.

"Hit the elevator button," Bear yelled.

Dylan pushed the button but then moved the three of them to the stairs.

"Whatcha doing, man?" Bear tried to pull Angelina back toward the elevator.

"We're taking the stairs. We can't be sure they're alone. Others might be riding up here right now. Don't want to be greeted with gunfire when the elevator door opens, do we?"

Bear pushed open the door to the stairwell and peered over the railing. "Are you crazy? It's ten floors."

"Getting soft in your old age, Simmons?"

"I'll give you 'getting soft.'" Bear almost growled the words.

Dylan chuckled in spite of the tension of the moment. Everybody knew Bear counted the days, hours and even the minutes until his retirement party in six months. He'd become a little less willing to risk any injury. But Dylan intended to make sure his partner made it to that party in one large cake-eating piece.

Dylan forced his mind into overdrive, doing a double and triple check of every decision he made. He vowed not to lose the life of a second partner on his watch like he'd done years ago.

"Dylan…"

Pure terror resonated in Angelina's voice yet her outward demeanor remained calm and collected.

"It's going to be all right, Angelina." He gave her noninjured arm a reassuring squeeze. "We've got you. We'll be out of here and safe in a few minutes. Don't worry."

He threw a glance over his right shoulder to make sure they weren't being followed. Then, offering a silent prayer that he was making the right decision, he nodded to his partner and they began their descent down the stairs.

Not a word passed between them as they moved in an even rhythm through the stairwell.

Angelina's head pounded with pain. Her blurred vision made the stairwell and the men beside her appear as if they were underwater. But she didn't dare complain. She couldn't be responsible for slowing them down when she knew every second was crucial to keeping the three of them alive.

Dylan grinned when they reached the ground floor. "We made it!"

"You sound surprised. That sigh of relief doesn't instill a great deal of confidence here, McKnight."

"What are you talking about? I told you it would be okay. I'd keep you safe." Dylan gingerly patted her shoulder. "And I will."

When Bear released Angelina's other arm, she slid to the bottom step, grateful for the moment of rest.

Bear leaned over, his huge hands bracing his upper body against his knees, and sucked air deeply into his lungs. "Yeah, well don't start celebrating yet," he baited Dylan. "All we've managed to do is jog down a million steps."

Angelina smiled up at the older man. "You did a good job. Thank you for keeping me safe."

A surprised expression crossed his face. Then he nodded almost shyly in acknowledgment of her compliment.

"Stop your griping, Bear." Dylan slapped his partner on the back. "You really are getting soft, you know. Good thing you'll be hanging up your shield soon. Those bones of yours are getting pretty old."

"Don't get too sure of yourself. How long do you think it's going to take the bad guys to figure out we took the stairs? A nanosecond from now?"

Dylan glanced up the stairwell and then out into the corridor. "My guess is they're riding the elevator and searching floor by floor."

Bear nodded. "Then let's get out of here before they

figure it out. I'm a bigger target than you. Today's not the day I feel like getting shot."

"Copy that, big guy."

Dylan helped Angelina rise from the step. "You okay?"

She nodded. But she knew Dylan wasn't blind. Her eyes watered from the pounding in her temples and she didn't know how much longer she could tolerate the pain.

Still, she couldn't slow them down. She refused to be the reason any more people died. Not today. Not ever.

"Beat you to the back door." She forced herself to grin at the two men.

"You're doing great." Dylan stared into her eyes exuding more confidence than she was sure he felt.

She knew she wasn't fooling him but he wasn't fooling her, either. They were in danger. Huge danger. And every second counted.

"One more corridor. Just one more," he assured her. "Selma's right on the other side of that last door and then we'll be safe."

Angelina took a deep breath. Now she understood what it meant when people said the spirit is willing but the flesh is weak. She knew her fighting spirit and determination wouldn't let her down but she worried that her body was another story.

"We'll do this together, Miss Baroni," Bear said, clasping her under the arm. "Let's go."

Without another word, both men picked her up and moved in a rapid pace toward that back door. She knew neither man would dare voice their own fears that Selma and the getaway car might not be there in time but tension was written all over their faces.

Excruciating pain pounded in her temples at each jolt of her body. Her vision blurred even more and nausea cramped her stomach.

Dear Lord.

The beginning of a prayer came naturally. It saddened her that she couldn't feel comfortable anymore talking to the Lord, the only One whom she had once believed could truly keep her safe, whom she had once sought for comfort and inner peace.

Angelina gritted her teeth and endured the ache in each arm as the men half carried, half dragged her down the corridor.

The men's pace increased almost with a desperation she knew they didn't want to show.

This wasn't going to work. These men would forfeit their lives trying to get her to the safe house and she would have more blood, more good lives lost, on her head. The murder she witnessed of a neighbor had started this whole thing. Then, the loss of Maria. Who would be next?

A moan of grief escaped her lips.

"Almost there, Angelina. Hang on."

Dylan's voice penetrated her consciousness. He'd misinterpreted her moan for pain. Well, it was pain. But it was so much more—fear, grief, uncertainty.

Please, please don't let anyone else die.

She couldn't help offering the prayer even though she truly believed God didn't listen to her anymore. Maybe this time He would. For these men if not for her.

She thought back to the night three years ago when she'd deceived Dylan. Funny thing, the mind. Here she was being shot at by mobsters and being dragged down corridors and all her mind wanted to think about was Dylan.

They'd gotten close…much closer than either of them had expected. Dylan had done his best to be professional and keep his personal feelings out of it. He'd even made jokes that it was nothing more than physical attraction blossoming between them and they needed to ignore it.

But she knew it had been more.

She'd touched his heart. She saw it in his eyes when he looked at her. She felt it in the warmth of his touch, a touch lasting a moment longer than it should. She heard it in the gentle huskiness of his voice when he spoke to her.

And she'd exploited those feelings.

A twinge of shame and regret hit her conscience. How could she have hurt him like that? Particularly when she hadn't been sure he had deceived her. His current actions made her more certain than ever that she'd misjudged him.

Now it was worse. Those gentle feelings she'd seen in his eyes years ago were replaced with anger, mistrust and pain. Yet here he was putting his life on the line to protect her, again. He was probably going to get himself killed. And it was all her fault.

"There they are!" Male voices at the distant end of the corridor rang out and were quickly following by the sound of feet pounding the floor.

"If you've ever said a prayer, man, this would be a good time to do it," Bear yelled to Dylan. Then he slammed the palm of his hand against the back door. "Be there. Be there. Be there."

The three of them paused on the loading dock, acclimating themselves to the darkness and to their surroundings.

"Hurry! Over here!" Selma's crisp, tense voice carried in the cool autumn air.

Angelina's body took another heavy jolt as the men sprang into action, lifted her feet off the ground, and ran with her bouncing between them toward the dark sedan barely visible in the poorly lit drive. The severe jarring motion made every muscle in her body scream in protest.

Her stomach roiled and it took all her strength to remain conscious.

Bear pulled open the back passenger door and dived in. He reached out his hand to pull her in after him. Dylan brought up the rear.

Angelina squinted as the bright light of the car interior hit her eyes, sending shafts of fresh pain through her eyes.

The sound of a bullet hitting metal made Dylan push her into the backseat. Her face mashed against Bear's chest. She could hear his voice reverberate against her ear as he yelled to Selma.

"Go! Go! Get out of here! Now!"

Sandwiched between Dylan and Bear, Angelina heard the car tires squeal before Dylan had even closed the back door.

Another bullet on metal. Then another.

"Stay down!" Dylan ordered, shoving her head deeper into Bear's chest as his large, ungainly partner sprawled half on and half off the backseat. Why was God letting this happen? Why wasn't He bringing her father to justice before more innocent people got hurt?

The car swayed to the right. Then Selma took a sharp turn to the left.

Angelina grabbed hold of Bear's shirt and tried to steady herself and not crash backward into Dylan.

Selma made another right-hand turn, this time down a backstreet. Angelina was certain they did it on two tires, not four, before the car banked sharply back to the left. They cut through an industrial park parking lot.

"I think you lost them. I don't think they were able to grab a car in time to follow us." Dylan, gun drawn, his back pressed against the back of the driver's seat and his knee digging painfully into Angelina's side as he balanced himself on the seat, pointed his weapon at the rear window.

"Where are we going?" Selma called from the front.

"Just get us out of here," Dylan yelled. "We'll figure it out when we're not dodging bullets."

"Roger that."

All three of them were thrown together as Selma hit the accelerator and took another sharp turn.

Angelina couldn't tolerate the pain in her head another second. Her blurred vision quickly became a sheet of black. She gave up the fight and slid into the welcome darkness.

"Angelina!" Dylan pulled her into his arms and cradled her head against his chest. "Open your eyes. Stay with us. C'mon, open those eyes." His heart pounded and the pulse in his temple throbbed. She had to be okay. She had to be.

He gently shook her. "Angelina. C'mon. Open your eyes."

"Maybe we ought to take her back to the hospital." Bear's solemn stare almost made Dylan lose it. His part-

ner never would suggest taking her back into danger
unless he thought she was going to die.

She wasn't going to die. Not here. Not now. He wouldn't
allow the thought to enter his mind.

C'mon, Lord. I need You now. Please, Lord.

Angelina's eyelids fluttered.

"That's a girl." Relief coated Dylan's every word.

A little more fluttering and then Angelina opened
her eyes and stared back at him. He'd never been more
grateful for anything.

"Good girl! Now take some deep breaths. Inhale
through your nose. C'mon, Angelina. Breathe in. That's
a girl. Now purse your lips and blow out slowly. Good
girl. Now do it again. Nice and slow. Again."

"My head." She lifted her fingers to touch her temple. "The pain…"

"I know. I'm sorry. Here." He placed two pills in
her hand. "The doctor gave me these. Take them. They
should help. I just need you to hang in there a little bit
longer. Can you do that for us?"

Selma reached over the front seat and handed back
a bottle of water.

Angelina started to nod but stopped instantly and
grimaced. Her fingers moved to her mouth. "I'm going
to be sick."

"I've got something for that, too." He handed her the
antinausea pills. "Just a little longer, Angelina. We're
almost there."

"Where?" Selma stage-whispered from the front
seat. "You never did tell me where I'm supposed to be
driving."

"I don't know." Dylan raised his head and looked

out the back window. They'd pulled into an alley when Angelina had lost consciousness. "Have we lost them?"

"I think so." Bear slid his gun back into his shoulder holster. "I haven't seen anyone for a while now."

Dylan returned his attention to the woman sprawled on the backseat. "That's it. Slow, deep breaths. Keep your eyes open. Just listen to my voice and blow the breath out slowly. In. Out. There you go."

He tapped the driver's headrest. "Just drive, Selma. Give us a few minutes to figure this out."

She nodded and turned the key in the ignition.

Dylan gathered Angelina in his arms. He held her tightly in the confined space in an attempt to steady her as much as possible as Selma pulled out of the alley.

Bear squished himself against the door and window in an attempt to give them space in the cramped quarters.

"I don't see anyone behind us." Selma and Dylan's eyes met in the rearview mirror. "We've lost them." Selma slowed the car and merged into normal traffic. "What do you want me to do now?"

"Find a diner or small restaurant. Something off the beaten path while we wait for the text on the location of the safe house. Angelina needs to rest. We need to call this in and all of us need to take a minute to unwind and regroup."

"Sounds good." Bear pulled a cell phone out of his pocket. "I'll call it in and find out what's the holdup on the safe house."

Dylan repositioned Angelina. For a moment when she'd blacked out he had thought he'd lost her. Panic had coursed through his veins. He couldn't afford to lose this witness. If she didn't testify, her father would walk free. That's what it was, worry about his witness.

His hands shook. He almost had to sit on them to refrain from brushing the hair off her face.

What was the matter with him? Why were his insides in a knot and his chest feeling as if he'd just had a major heart attack when he saw her slip into unconsciousness?

She was an important witness. Nothing more. That's all she was.

He looked down at her long lashes wet with tears as she closed her eyes and burrowed in his arms.

Yeah, right. Just a witness.

Who did he think he was kidding?

FIVE

Bear supported one arm and Dylan the other as the three of them followed Selma into the restaurant. Angelina's feet didn't seem to want to hold her weight. She stumbled and dragged them and was grateful for the men's support. It took a moment for her eyes to adjust to the change in lighting, which was much dimmer inside than outside. The establishment had strategically placed candles and amber glowing lanterns to light the pathways and tables. Probably to create an air of romance or intimacy but Angelina didn't care why, she was just happy that glaring sunlight wasn't hitting her eyes and exacerbating the pain in her head. The pills Dylan had given her in the car were beginning to take effect. The pain was manageable. The nausea ceased and the aroma of grilled steaks actually made her stomach growl.

When they stood at the hostess stand in the foyer, the hostess took one look at the two men literally holding Angelina up and then locked gaze with her. Angelina had thrown clothes from Selma's car on over her hospital gown, but it did little to help with her disheveled appearance, bandages and bruises. The hostess's wary demeanor and hesitancy couldn't conceal her curiosity. "Is everything all right?"

Angelina forced a smile on her face. "Everything will be fine as long as those steaks taste as good as they smell."

Dylan sent her an appreciative smile. He probably didn't feel like making up excuses or explanations for nosy hostesses.

The woman smiled, picked out four menus, silverware wrapped in white linen, and said, "Follow me."

The four of them slid into a booth, accepted their menus and within minutes had placed their drink orders with the waitress.

When the waitress stepped away, Dylan lowered his menu and looked at Angelina, concern evident in his expression. "How are you holding up? Have the meds helped?"

Angelina started to nod and caught herself in time. Nope. No moving her head if she could help it. Instead she simply smiled. "I'm starving. That's a good sign, right? And since the feds are picking up the tab, I'm going to order the biggest and most expensive steak on the menu."

Bear chuckled. "Great idea. Sign me up."

Dylan grinned at both of them. He perused the menu, taking time to make his own meal selection but he didn't fool Angelina. His gaze had located all entries and exits from the moment they'd hit the foyer until they'd been seated. His senses, on high alert, sprang to attention with every person coming anywhere near their table. His gaze noted every new customer walking through the door. At this rate, the poor man would never get anything to eat.

"Dylan, relax." She smiled at him again but even mere smiles were quickly becoming taxing and tiring. The past twenty-four hours seemed like a nightmare that wouldn't stop.

"She's right, partner. I kept an eagle eye and nobody followed us. We're okay for the moment."

"I agree." Selma stood. "I'm going to the ladies' room." She glanced at Angelina. "Do you need to come?"

Angelina shook her head no and winced.

Selma pulled out her cell phone and looked at Dylan. "I'll step outside and make contact with the boss. They must have the safe house ready by now and I want to see if there have been any new developments on the case."

Dylan nodded his approval. "What do you want me to order for you?"

Selma gestured with the phone toward Bear. "Half the size of whatever you order for him. You see what large portions cause."

Bear grumbled and everyone at the table chuckled as Selma left.

The three of them engaged in idle conversation when suddenly Bear stilled. His partner's stoic expression and sudden ramrod posture instantly alerted Dylan to a potential problem.

"What?" He kept his voice low and quickly glanced over his shoulder in the direction of Bear's gaze.

"I know that guy."

"Who?"

"White hair. Black windbreaker. Just sat down at the bar."

Dylan dropped his napkin on the floor, bent to pick it up, and used the opportunity to look in the man's direction. When he came back up, his mouth formed a grim frown. "That's Joey Bitters."

"Yep. Small world isn't it?"

Angelina glanced back and forth between the two men. The tension between them made goose bumps raise on her flesh. "Who is Joey Bitters?"

"He's a low-level thug in your father's organization." Dylan threw his napkin on the table. "Let's get out of here."

"Whoa, hold up." Bear loosened a button on his jacket and slid his hand inside. "Could be a coincidence. We're not that far from the city. People do come to restaurants to eat. Even thugs."

Dylan's frown deepened, carving deep worry lines into his face. He didn't seem to like this new turn of events, not at all.

"Dylan?" Angelina's heart beat double time. Had they been followed? Was Dylan right? Now that she was back in protective custody, had her father put a contract out on her life?

Dylan didn't respond. Instead, he leaned his left arm over the back of the booth. To an innocent bystander he appeared casual and laid-back. But Angelina noted the way his jacket hung open. Saw his gun nestled in his shoulder harness. Knew in this position he could draw his weapon in an instant.

She had to get out of here.

Frantically her gaze darted around the room in search of the nearest exit. Her mind ping-ponged with one poor scenario after another as she tried to plan her escape. She couldn't let these men be killed while trying to protect her.

She glanced at the other patrons.

And all these innocent people, simply out to dinner with their friends or family members. How could she live with herself if anything happened to any of them?

She placed her hands against the edge of the table and prepared to push and run when Bear's voice caught her attention.

"See? Nothing to worry about."

Dylan dared another glance in that direction and so did she.

A woman with big hair, bleached blond and piled up like a bad wig, sat down beside the man at the bar. The woman, poured into a dress that left little to the imagination, stretched out an index finger to Mr. Thug's chin and leaned forward giving him a clear look at her cleavage.

"That's Vinnie Salvo's wife. Seems like Joey is dipping his toe in someone else's water. No wonder they're meeting out here in nowhere's land." Bear removed his hand from his jacket, took a swig of his soda and relaxed. "Nothing to do with us. Let's eat and get out of here."

Dylan sighed loudly. "I don't like it."

"I don't, either, but I'm not walking away from a free steak dinner because a nobody thug has the same taste in food as me."

Angelina watched the pair at the bar. Unless both of them were superb actors, they were so into each other they didn't have eyes for anyone or anything else. Bear was right. Eat and leave. Fast.

Still…

"The safe house is ready." Selma slid back into the booth. "The boss texted the address to all three of us. Check your phones."

Dylan and Bear did.

"Tom's River?" Dylan asked.

"Actually, Lanoka Harbor, which is just outside of Tom's River. I took the liberty to do a Google satellite search," Selma said. "We'll be sitting smack-dab in the middle of an average middle-class neighborhood. No one will think to look for us there."

"That's not like the boss. He usually picks someplace remote and private."

The waitress arrived with their food and their conversation was put on hold. When she'd left, Dylan leaned toward Bear and stage-whispered, "Does this feel right to you? First the low-life thug showing up and now a safe house that is anywhere but safe?"

"What thug?" Selma twisted her head to look around the room.

Bear dived into his steak. "Short notice. Boss did the best he could." Between chews he gestured with his fork in Joey's direction. "And I don't care what you say, that guy over there only has one thing on his mind and it ain't us."

Angelina listened quietly to the conversation as she ate her food. Despite twinges of nausea, she enjoyed every bite. She hadn't eaten since yesterday's celebratory dinner and she was hungry.

Thoughts about that dinner and everything that had happened since threatened to steal her appetite away but she knew she had to keep up her strength if she was going to be able to go through with her plans. She needed to escape. She needed to save these people… and herself. But how? She could barely walk on her own two feet let alone run.

Angelina shot frequent glances at the two people sitting at the bar. She had to agree with Bear. Whoever that guy was, the only thing that seemed to be on his mind was finishing his drink and getting a room. She doubted he had anything to do with them. Some of the tension left her body. As for the safe house, she was glad it was in a middle-class neighborhood and not a remote, isolated location. It would be easier for her to slip away.

And she would slip away…the very first chance she got.

Dylan could have been eating shoe leather for all the appeal his dinner had. His gut remained clenched and his senses jumped at every sudden sound or unexpected movement. Not one to believe in coincidences, although he knew they happened to people every day, he had to admit the thug at the bar didn't seem to be an immediate threat.

He was sure there was an arrest warrant out there for the guy but Dylan wasn't concerned with contacting the local police. Dylan had a feeling when Vinnie Salvo discovered his wife was two-timing him with Joey, the consequences would be stiffer than any slap on the wrist the law could impose. Sometimes you just had to sit back and let things happen on their own.

Dylan finished as much of his meal as he could manage and pushed the plate away.

Thank God, Angelina looked better. Taking the medication and getting some food seemed to be doing her a world of good. She had color in her cheeks again. The dark shadows of pain beneath her eyes lightened. He sighed heavily. This was going to be the toughest six days of his life—or five and a half days, now. But he'd do it. He'd keep Angelina safe and he'd get her into the courtroom no matter what.

It was the "what" he'd have to do that worried him.

Selma slid her cell phone across the table toward Angelina. "Does this man look familiar to you?"

Dylan leaned forward for a quick look and shot a questioning glance at Selma.

Angelina picked up the phone and studied the picture. "I'm not sure. Should he?"

This new information grabbed Dylan's attention. What was going on? Who was the person in the picture? Where had Selma gotten it? And why hadn't she shared it with him or Bear prior to showing it to a witness?

"His name is Frankie Malone." Selma folded her hands on the table and waited.

Angelina studied the photo harder. "Yeah. Now I remember." She glanced up at Selma. "Maria dated him. I only met him once so that's why I didn't recognize him right away."

"What can you tell us about him?"

Angelina thought for a moment. "Not much, I'm afraid. She dated him for a few months. Talked about him all the time but, truthfully, nothing special or specific. Things like how handsome he was…or how thoughtful…or how hot." Angelina grinned at the memory. "She was crazy about the guy."

"Nothing else?" Selma stared hard at her. "And you only met him the one time? Even though Maria was your best friend and she was crazy about him?" Selma shrugged. "Your words, right?"

"What's going on?" Dylan pierced Selma with a look but she ignored him.

"Nothing. I'm just wondering why our witness

doesn't know more about her best friend's special guy. After all, you roomed together. You'd think you had to be home once in a while when the guy came to pick her up for a date."

"I don't know why I didn't see more of him." Angelina shrugged. "I guess I was preoccupied with our advertising agency and wasn't paying much attention to Maria's private life. He never came inside the apartment. He'd always pull the car up front, beep, and she'd go out."

"Didn't you find that behavior strange for such a 'great' guy?"

"Like I said, I didn't think about it at all." Angelina squirmed under Selma's intense scrutiny. "Besides the relationship didn't last long, anyway."

"What happened?"

"I don't know. Once things started to sour, Maria kept pretty quiet. She didn't want to talk about it and I respected her privacy. They stopped seeing each other about three or four weeks ago. Broke Maria's heart but she was working her way through it. The advertising contract we got the other night made her happier than I'd seen her in weeks."

Angelina slid the phone back to Selma. "Why are you asking about Frankie?"

All eyes at the table focused on Selma.

"Because it's beginning to look like he might have been responsible for killing Maria."

Bear choked and almost spit out his mouthful of coffee. He swallowed hard and then said, "What? Who says so? When did all of this happen?"

"Frankie killed Maria?" Angelina's eyes widened like a deer in headlights. "Do you mean I wasn't the target? That Frankie was after Maria? That my dad hasn't put out a contract on me?"

"Wait a minute. What's going on?" Dylan grabbed the phone from Selma, took a long hard look at the photo and then handed it back. "Explain, Selma. And make it good."

Selma tucked the phone in her purse. "When I checked in with the boss a few minutes ago about the safe house, he sent me this picture and told me to show it to Angelina and see what I could find out. Seems they have a witness who saw this man running away from the area beneath the pier."

"Nice of you to tell us." Dylan's tone left no doubt he was annoyed to be getting this information after the fact.

"Sorry, Dylan. I received it only a few minutes ago." Selma looked at Angelina. "I didn't want to show it to you in front of her. I wanted to catch her off guard and get an honest reaction to the picture."

"Thanks." Angelina's sarcastic tone didn't impact Selma at all.

"What did you expect?" Selma asked. "You're the daughter of an organized crime boss. Do you really expect us to treat you like you're Miss Sweet and Innocent because you've agreed to testify against your father? If I read the records correctly, you stuck it to us and disappeared for three years. Doesn't put you high in the trustworthy category in my book."

"Selma! Knock it off!"

"It's all right, Dylan." Angelina held up her palm to stop him. "She's right. None of us knows whether we can trust one another or not. My father has a long reach. He owns judges, cops—probably federal marshals." She paused, allowing them to process that information. When she looked at Dylan her eyes revealed pain, held an unanswered question he didn't understand. "It's probably a good idea for all of us to proceed with the notion that no one can be trusted. No surprises that way. That's what I'm going to do."

Dylan winced. Why had her words hurt him? Why did he care one way or the other whether she trusted him or not?

But he did.

"Okay, children, let's wrap this family argument up and get ourselves out of here." Bear stood, threw his napkin on the table and shrugged in the direction of Joey Bitters. "Our friend just got company. One thug in the same place as me is one too many. Four thugs tell me to exit stage left."

Dylan glanced toward the bar. He raised his eyebrow when he saw Vinnie Salvo and two of his goons saunter toward the couple still sitting at the bar.

Yep, time to get out of Dodge.

SIX

Dylan stood on the sidewalk in front of the assigned safe house and surveyed the neighborhood. He understood why his superiors had thought this house would work. The house to their left sat empty. The dilapidated condition of the house and lawn told Dylan no one had been by the residence in a considerable time. The for-sale sign in the yard looked worn, old and dirty.

The vinyl-sided house they would be staying in backed up to woods and had a six-foot privacy fence in the backyard. There was no house on the right, just more woods. The middle-class neighborhood looked like any other middle-class neighborhood. Intel reported that most of the homes on this block were occupied by working parents with school-aged children. The streets would most likely be quiet and empty during the day and since it got dark early in October, empty at night, as well.

Yes, this would be a satisfactory safe house.

Dylan finished installing the small camera on the mailbox post that would target the street. He'd already put one by the front door to provide a video of anyone coming or going as well as one on each side of the house and two in the back. The ones in the back would focus on the approach to the back door as well as any movement over the fence. Bear was already inside monitoring them.

Dylan looked once more up and down the street.

Nothing threatening. Nothing suspicious. Good.

The brisk October air bit his cheeks and ears. The slight breeze rustled the leaves, several falling to the ground at his feet as he watched. He'd always loved autumn's beauty, the last glorious blast of life before the cold fingers of wintry death claimed the land. He only hoped he'd be able to prevent the cold fingers of death from touching any of them.

Two more marshals would be arriving at six in the morning to spell Bear and Selma. They'd work in shifts twelve hours on and twelve off.

Dylan already informed his boss that he intended to remain 24/7 at the house. Since he'd lost this witness once before, his boss understood his need to see this job through personally to a successful conclusion.

Bear had opted to take his relief at the house as well and grab some shut-eye in one of the many bedrooms. Dylan grinned. He hadn't been surprised. His partner had never left him in the lurch and wasn't about to start now. Dylan wondered what he was going to do when Bear retired. He wasn't sure he wanted to try and adjust to a new partner. Maybe it was time for Dylan to find a different line of work, too.

A black SUV turned the corner and slowly rolled down the street.

Dylan tensed and watched the vehicle, knowing that Bear also saw the approach on video cam and would be ready if backup was necessary.

The SUV swung into the driveway of a house three doors down. Almost as soon as the engine cut off, the doors opened and what appeared to be a father and his young son jumped out and headed directly into the house.

Dylan relaxed.

He took one final glance around the neighborhood. Satisfied they were safe for the night, he sprinted for the front door.

Once inside, he immediately went in search of Angelina. He found her exactly where he thought she would be, in the den, curled up in front of the fireplace with a book. Selma, sitting on the sofa opposite her, appeared engrossed in a magazine article.

When Angelina heard Dylan approach, she closed the book. "Everything okay?"

Dylan nodded and plopped down on the chair across from her.

"I have something I want to talk to you about."

He spread his arms along the back of the upholstered chair.

"Shoot." Immediately, he grimaced.

Way to go, stupid. Great word choice. That will make her feel relaxed.

Angelina glanced at Selma, who was peering at them over the top of her magazine, and then turned her attention back to Dylan.

"Is it true?" Angelina folded her hands in her lap. "That Frankie killed Maria out of revenge for breaking up with him? Is it possible my father had nothing to do with her death or my getting shot?"

Dylan couldn't stand the hope he saw in her expression. Why did she still harbor feelings for this man? He didn't care if he was her father or not. He was a capo, a cold-blooded, heartless criminal. And yet she still cared about him.

He just couldn't understand it.

He'd been raised in foster homes most of his life. This loyalty and devotion was alien to him. The only time he'd felt unconditional, undying love was when he'd spent time with God. He hadn't seen much of it in the human population.

"I don't know. But does it really matter whether he did it or not? It doesn't matter whether there is one shooter out there or if your father hired a hundred shooters. We still have to keep you hidden and safe for the next few days. We can't take any unnecessary chances, can we?"

Selma placed the magazine on the end table and stood up. "I'm going into the kitchen and get a mug of hot chocolate." She smiled at Angelina. "Would you like some?"

Angelina nodded.

Selma glanced over at Dylan. "Do you want anything?"

"No, but thanks for asking."

After she'd left, Dylan turned his attention back to Angelina.

"What is it? What's really troubling you?"

"I want to know more about this man, Frankie. Who is he? What does he do for a living? Where on earth did Maria meet him?" Angelina frowned. "I should have questioned her more about him but she seemed so happy and I didn't want to pry. I figured she'd tell me what she wanted me to know when she wanted me to know it."

She wiped an errant tear from her cheek. "Maybe she'd still be alive if I'd pushed a little harder to find out what was going wrong between them."

"You can't blame yourself for this. It wasn't your fault."

"Dylan's right." Selma handed her a mug of chocolate and plopped back down on the sofa. "You met the guy once, right? How were you supposed to know he worked for your father?"

Angelina startled. "He worked for my father? Are you sure?"

"I can't figure you out." Selma tilted her head and studied Angelina as if she were an interesting species of bug. "Frankie sells drugs out of an Atlantic City gang. He has a rap sheet as long as your arm. He's a criminal."

"Selma…" Dylan's tone warned her to go easy but she didn't stop.

"All the criminals—the loan sharks, the enforcers, the drug runners—they all work for organized crime. Vincenzo Baroni *is* organized crime in the state of New Jersey. Who did you think Frankie worked for?"

Angelina paled as the truth of Selma's words hit her full force.

"I guess… I…well, I never thought…"

"That's what I just can't figure out, yet. But I will."

"What do you mean?" Angelina looked clearly puzzled.

"Are you really that naive? Or are you sly like a fox and trying to play us?"

"Selma, that's enough." Dylan's sharp tone brought the conversation to a halt.

Selma shrugged. She looked directly at Angelina. "If it's true that you thought your father was some do-gooder businessman, a true pillar in the community, then I suppose this must have been a pretty hard blow for you. I'm not trying to make you feel worse."

Angelina accepted her nonapology apology with a silent nod.

"I'm going up to bed and try to catch a couple of hours' sleep so I can spell Bear. He's in the kitchen watching the monitors…and his news channel on the countertop television. Guess the guy thinks the world will stop if he isn't paying attention to current events. Me, I have plenty of current events doing this job. I don't have to live them 24/7. Different strokes for different folks, I suppose."

Selma caught Angelina's eye. "If it's true, if you didn't know who and what your father was…who he still is… then I feel sorry for you. I really do."

She stood and placed her empty cocoa mug down. "Good people are putting their lives on the line for you. Again. I read your file. I know you ran out on us three years ago. Gave Dylan's career a black eye and almost caused us to lose this case."

"Selma, she's been through enough. Leave her alone," Dylan said.

Selma raised her arm in a gesture of surrender. "Okay, okay, I'm going upstairs." She pierced Angelina with her stare. "I don't know why Bear and Dylan think you're worth a second chance. I don't trust you as far as I can throw you and I'm going to be watching every move you make. Just want you to know that." She nodded Dylan's way. "Good night."

"I'm sorry. She was pretty harsh."

Angelina shrugged.

"She was right. I do have good people putting their lives on the line for me. And I did run away before." She looked him right in the eye. "And I will do it again the very first chance I get."

A pained expression crossed his face. "Then you'll understand if we don't give you any opportunity to do it."

An uncomfortable silence descended upon them. She stared at the fire and searched for a way to turn the conversation to less awkward ground.

If she could only make him understand...

Angelina didn't know who to trust. She didn't know what to do. She only knew she didn't want any further loss of life on her hands, particularly Dylan's and Bear's, and she didn't know how to stop it. She hoped Frankie was the shooter. Then the shooting wouldn't be connected to her father and these US marshals who were trying to protect her would be safe.

Dylan picked up her empty mug. "Would you like a refill?"

"No. Thank you, though."

"Why don't you go up and lie down? You certainly need the rest."

"I'm not tired."

"That's good, I guess." Dylan grinned. "At least I won't have to be worried about a concussion. Doc said with a concussion you'd want to sleep."

Dylan moved closer. "Angelina..." He waited until he had her attention.

"You are going to testify, aren't you? You aren't really planning to run away again, are you? Make me understand."

Unbidden tears, from pain, from exhaustion, from

emotions, flowed down her cheeks in a nonending stream. She wiped her hand across her cheeks.

"I'm going to testify. But that doesn't mean I am going to stay in custody until the trial. It's dangerous—for everyone—and if I get a chance to leave, I will take it. I'm just being honest."

"But you don't want to testify against Vincenzo, do you? Even after what you saw your father do?"

Angelina offered him a smile but it held no happiness or joy. "Sometimes, Dylan, I think this entire situation has all been a terrible nightmare and if I wait long enough I'll wake up." She knew she couldn't hide the pain in her voice. "But I just can't seem to wake up."

She looked into his deep, brown eyes and saw compassion and patience while he waited for her to continue.

"My father was a good father. You know my mother died from pneumonia when I was barely two. My father was the only parent I knew. He'd cuddle with me every night and read me bedtime stories until I fell asleep. He'd come home from work…" Her eyes caught his. "The work I thought was a regular job like all the other dads had—and he'd play with me. He had an iron-clad rule, only one video game a night before dinner. He'd sit with me after dinner and help me with my homework. When I hit high school, it was my father who taught me how to dance so I'd be ready for my prom. It was my father…it was always my father…who taught me how to love." Angelina choked on her sobs.

Dylan handed her a box of tissues. She wiped her tears away and blew her nose.

"I'll never forget the look on his face the day I came home from school and told him what you had said to me."

Dylan raised an eyebrow in question but didn't interrupt her.

"It was the beginning of sixth grade. Do you remember?"

Dylan frowned. "I had a schoolboy crush on you. I remember that."

Angelina shook her head. "You had overheard your parents talking about my dad. I don't think you even understood the significance of what you said to me. I know I didn't." She chuckled and blew her nose again. "We were so innocent back then. So foolish."

She looked into Dylan's eyes and saw the flash of memory as it all came pouring back for both of them.

"You asked me to go to the movies with you. I told you I couldn't because my dad wouldn't let me. You got mad and said you'd ask me again after my dad went to jail because he was a bad man. He belonged to the mafia and the police were going to arrest him and put him away for life."

Dylan's cheeks flamed as the memory of those childhood words flooded over him.

"I was mad at you," she said, a genuine grin shining through her tears. "I realize you were just repeating something you heard the adults in your life say but it hurt. I ran home and told my father. I asked him what the mafia was and if the police were going to arrest him."

Dylan looked ill. "That's why I never saw you again."

"My father assured me you were making up crazy, mean stories and he shipped me off to a private boarding school. After that, I only saw my father for holidays and school breaks." Her eyes met his. "And I never saw you again...until the police chief walked me into the US

Marshal's office for protection after I'd reported that I had seen my father kill a man."

"Angelina…"

Dylan gathered her in his arms and cradled her against his chest. "I am so sorry."

She could feel the warmth of his body. She could hear the beat of his heart. She could hear the rumbling of his voice in his chest when he spoke.

And she let him comfort her.

For this tiny instant in time, she needed someone to comfort her and try to push away her pain. She needed someone to understand she hated his actions, absolutely hated them—but she could still love the man. He was her father.

"Ahem." Bear stood awkwardly in the doorway.

Angelina and Dylan jumped apart.

She hated the chagrined, embarrassed look that appeared on Dylan's face. He couldn't even meet her eyes.

"What's up, Bear?" Dylan asked.

"Hate to break things up in here." Bear gestured with his head to the front door. "But we've got company."

Dylan withdrew his gun from his shoulder harness. He looked at Angelina, put a finger across his lips to silence her and gestured for her to stay put.

He glanced through the curtain. A black SUV, looking just like the one he'd seen earlier, parked in their driveway. After cutting the engine, a solitary man, about five-ten, wearing denim jeans and a baseball windbreaker stepped out of the car and approached the house.

Dylan followed Bear to the front door and, with gun

drawn, stepped to the side out of sight, nodding the okay for his partner to answer the bell.

Bear swung the door open halfway. "Can I help you?"

"Hi! My name's Travis Holden. I live three houses down on the left."

Bear smiled politely but didn't open the door wider or offer to let the man enter.

"Anyway, I saw a man outside by the mailbox a few hours ago. We were surprised to see anybody here. Old Man Tillman lives alone. He mentioned he'd be away for a month or so visiting family. So we were wondering…"

Dylan studied the man through the slight opening between the door and jamb. He seemed unsure of himself and definitely uncomfortable. His eyes shifted frequently. He had a hard time making eye contact with Bear. He kept shuffling his feet and didn't seem to know what to do with his hands.

"Anyway, my wife wouldn't shut up about it. You know how wives can get sometimes." The man grinned and tried to include Bear in his joke. "She wouldn't rest until I came up here and checked on things." The man strained his neck and tried to peer past Bear, which almost made Dylan laugh. Trying to see past Bear would be like trying to glance over a mountain.

"So, is everything okay here?" Dylan again tried to refrain from laughing at the sheepish expression on the neighbor's face.

Bear laughed and reached out to shake the man's hand. "Well, you tell your wife that she has a keen eye and that Mr. Tillman will be real pleased to hear that the two of you are watching out for his place while he's gone. My friend and I are real estate developers.

We've known Tillman for years. He mentioned that he would be out of town for a couple of months visiting relatives. We offered to rent the place while we're in town finishing up our business. It's a win-win for both of us. Gives him a little cash to supplement his retirement and helps us out. Staying in hotels can get old after a while."

The neighbor grinned and shook Bear's hand. "See. I told her there was a reasonable explanation. So how long are you guys gonna be in town?"

"Can't say for sure. You know how business deals go. Could be a couple of weeks or more. But if we're lucky, we'll finish up and be out of here in a couple of days. Either way, our friend Tillman got a month's rent and my friend's wife is providing us with home-cooked meals instead of fast-food joints while we finish our business."

"So there's a woman here, too?" Again, the man tried to peer around Bear.

"A couple of them." Bear winked. "My gal hit the hay already and to be truthful, man, I'm a bit tired myself." He dropped his hold on the neighbor's hand. "But thanks again for stopping by. Appreciate it. Good night."

The neighbor grinned, waved and headed back to his truck.

Dylan watched the truck pull out of the driveway and continued to watch until he saw it pull into the driveway three doors down.

"Stupid man." Bear poked fun at the neighbor. "Er, um, are you a burglar, man?" He shook his head in disgust. "If I was a bad guy, didn't he think I could have blown his head off?" He closed the door. "I'll call it in," he said and headed back to the kitchen.

Dylan rejoined Angelina in the den. He saw the panic in her eyes and hurried to reassure her. "Nosy neighbor. Nosy wife. Nothing to worry about."

Angelina exhaled deeply and Dylan wondered if she'd been holding her breath the entire time.

Their eyes met and an awkward moment passed between them as they remembered what they'd been doing before Bear appeared in the doorway.

"Thanks for listening to me." Angelina couldn't meet his eyes.

"No problem. We're all here to make things as easy for you as possible."

Angelina gave him a telling glance.

He wasn't fooling her. What had passed between them had been anything but a simple comforting gesture from one federal marshal to a spooked witness and they both knew it.

"Well, thanks for listening, anyway. I appreciate it." She stood. "I am feeling a little tired after all. I think I'll go up and get some sleep. What room should I use?"

"The first door on the left. Selma and you are bunking together."

Angelina grinned. "Of course, we are."

Dylan watched her climb the stairs and disappear inside the bedroom.

What was wrong with him?

He never should have touched her. Never should have held her in his arms. Never should have comforted her.

Now he had to go into the kitchen and try to explain to Bear that he hadn't really seen what he thought he'd seen. And have a logical explanation when his partner asked him what was going on.

But how was he going to explain what he didn't understand himself?

SEVEN

Angelina rubbed the sleep from her eyes and stopped dead in her tracks in the entrance to the kitchen. Two people she'd never seen before were perched on stools and drinking coffee. She rubbed her eyes again.

The female, blonde, dressed in jeans and a T-shirt, jumped up and came to greet her. She held out her hand. "Hi. I'm Marshal Donna Clark. This is my partner, Brad Peterson."

The marshal stood and nodded his greeting. Angelina did a quick study. Brown hair. Brown eyes. Average build. Average height. Nothing notable, and that's probably one of the things that made him a good marshal. He could blend in to any assignment without being noticed.

"We're going to be your day detail today," Donna said.

Angelina shook her hand, only then noticing the small gun holster strapped to the woman's belt.

"Hi."

Donna herded Angelina to the kitchen table. "Would you like a cup of coffee? We just put on a fresh pot."

"Sure. Thanks. But I can get it myself. I don't expect you to wait on me."

That quickly, Donna was already across the room. "No problem. I'm up. And, yes, you will be free to get your own coffee and your own breakfast from here on out." She plunked a mug of steaming brew in front of her. "But I'm being nice."

"Believe me, that won't last long." Brad grinned at her. "This is probably the only cup of coffee I've seen her get anyone. You must be special."

Donna moved the creamer and sugar in front of her.

"Naw. You're not special. But Dylan told me that Selma was a little rough on you last night."

"Where are they?" Angelina swiveled her head back and forth.

"Selma headed out about an hour ago. She'll be back about six tonight." Brad winked at her. "That should give you plenty of time to put on armor for round two. Selma has a reputation for being tough." Brad put down his cup. "But she's a good marshal. She'll protect you with her life. Plus Bear will be staying at the house when his shift ends. He'll act as a buffer if you need one."

That's the trouble. I don't want any of you putting your life on the line for me.

"I must have been sleeping pretty soundly. I never heard her leave our room." Angelina took a sip of her coffee. Then trying to appear nonchalant she smiled at Brad. "And Dylan?"

"Dylan is right behind you."

The deep tenor of his voice washed over her and sent a wave of warmth through her body. She couldn't stop a grin from breaking out on her face when she turned his way. She shouldn't be this happy to see him. *I'm trying to find a way to escape him. Remember?*

"Good morning."

He stood in the doorway of the kitchen, finishing the last button on his shirt, his hair still damp from a shower. He looked fresh and clean and devastatingly handsome.

Angelina remembered the scent he wore and wondered how it mingled with fresh soap. She had to fight with herself to stay seated and not move closer to find out.

"I'm surprised you're still here." She picked up her cup and took another sip of coffee, more to give her hands something to do than because she was thirsty. "Isn't this your relief, too?"

Dylan came and stood beside her. His nearness was almost her undoing.

"I'm here for the duration. So is Bear. These marshals are in charge during the day. Bear will be back at night to help Selma during the night shift."

Angelina glanced at the clock. "You couldn't have gotten much sleep."

"Dylan can rest while we're gone." Donna stepped between them and perched a hip on one of the stools. "You better grab some breakfast if you're hungry. We need to leave here about nine."

Angelina blinked a couple of times. "Leave? Where are we going?"

"The US Attorney is meeting us in Atlantic City."

Angelina's chest tightened.

"He asked us to bring you in about ten."

"Why?" She didn't want to go into Atlantic City. She didn't want to leave the safety of this house...at least, not with them. She'd planned on spending her day trying to figure out a way to evade their protection completely.

"He's going to prepare you for your testimony." Donna perched on a stool beside her. "Don't worry. It's standard procedure. I'll bet ten bucks with anyone in this room that we'll be in and out in less than an hour. Any takers?"

"I don't gamble." Dylan poured a cup of coffee.

"You gamble every day only you bet your life instead of your money." Her tone showed her annoyance that neither he nor Brad had taken her up on her bet. "Anyway…" She turned her attention back to Angelina. "The DA will go over the questions he's going to ask you in court so there are no surprises. He wants you to be as comfortable as possible so the defense team can't make you nervous or trick you into saying something you don't intend to say."

Brad winked at her again. Maybe it was his idea of breaking the ice or something. She thought it foolish and a little bit annoying. His words made her realize he mistook her frown for fear.

"Don't worry. It'll be a piece of cake. You'll be so sick of hearing and answering the same questions over and over that you'll be able to do it in your sleep."

"That's right," Donna said. "We have a session with him both today and tomorrow. Then we have the weekend off to chill and relax before the big event. Maybe we can play a game of cards or Scrabble. Or we can rent a few romantic comedies and torture the guys. What do you think?"

Angelina's stomach twisted into a tight, painful knot. This was Thursday. The trial was only days away. If her father was going to make a move, then he would have to make it soon.

Her thoughts flew to Frankie. Was it possible Frankie had been the shooter Tuesday night? Maybe her father didn't know yet that she'd been found. Maybe he didn't know she was back in protective custody.

A heaviness cloaked her entire body.

Her father didn't reach his position of power without knowing *everything*.

"Oh, honey, relax. It'll be okay." Donna patted her hand reassuringly. "You'll probably be the first witness called Monday morning. Then this whole thing will be over. In the meantime, we promise to take real good care of you."

That's exactly what Angelina feared. That the marshals would do anything to keep her safe — even forfeit their own lives.

Angelina looked from one marshal to another. She liked Donna. She was sweet, thoughtful. Even wink-heavy Brad wasn't a bad guy. Maybe she was wrong about him. Maybe it wasn't a conceited wink. Maybe the poor guy had a tic. The thought made her grin.

She'd heard Bear snoring through the upstairs hall when she'd come out of her room. She remembered teasing him years ago about that snore. Apparently he, like Dylan, had chosen to stay for the duration.

And then, of course, there was dear old Selma.

Angelina couldn't find fault with Selma, either. She'd been right with everything she said. She'd betrayed them once before. Why should they trust her now?

A sadness, a heavy feeling of helplessness threatened to overwhelm her.

She knew her father. His life was on the line. He

had to find her. He had to stop her. And there was no question that he would. The only question was when and how.

But Angelina had her own plans. She fully intended to show up in court and testify on Monday morning. In the meantime, she was going to do everything in her power to ensure that there were no dead marshals left in the wake when her father did make his move to try and stop her.

Her eyes flew around the room and then her gaze locked on Dylan. The intensity in his stare told her he knew she was up to something.

Yep. Dylan would be her hardest challenge. She'd duped him once. How was she going to do it again? He'd be watching her every move.

She forced her body to relax. She didn't want him to pick up on any excess tension or his radar would take over. She smiled at him and took another sip of her coffee.

His eyes squinted and a deep frown line creased his forehead.

She had to be careful. She had already raised his suspicions. She had to find a way to fool him again. And, yes, it would probably end his career and he would hate her for it.

But at least he'd be alive. And that realization made any doubts or second thoughts she might have about slipping away disappear.

She couldn't allow anything to happen to Dylan.

She didn't question her feelings or dare to ask herself why she cared. It didn't matter. She'd do whatever she needed to do to keep him alive.

She needed a plan.

* * *

"Dylan, you shouldn't have come. We could have handled this. You're going to be exhausted tonight." Donna, sitting beside him in the front seat of the car, chastised him for the hundredth time that day.

"I'll be fine."

"Sure. With what? Two or three hours' sleep from last night? I'm sure glad you're not protecting me."

Dylan's hands gripped the steering wheel tightly so he wouldn't have the urge to grip her throat. "Knock it off, Donna. I'm fine. I got enough sleep and if I find myself getting tired tonight, I can catnap on the sofa. Bear and Selma will be on duty. Remember? So drop it."

Donna raised her hands in a gesture of surrender. "Okay, subject dropped. I'm just saying we could have handled this detail without your help. It's pretty routine you know."

"Yeah," Brad called from the backseat. "Like I told Angelina, it was a piece of cake."

Dylan glanced into the rearview mirror. Angelina lowered her head and placed her hand over her lips to hide the snicker he saw. Apparently, Brad wasn't winning Romeo points with their witness and a certain satisfaction curled in the pit of his stomach.

Things had gone well, today.

The DA had thrown every possible scenario at her. Asked her the same questions over and over to the point of almost being harassment. Raised his voice. Tried to intimidate her. Tried to twist her words and throw her off her game.

Nothing worked.

Angelina remained cool, calm and collected. Her

voice never wavered. Her story never changed. He was proud of her.

Now, if she could keep it together when she came face-to-face with her father in the courtroom, they'd be home free.

He had to admit he was worried about that little detail.

After their talk last night, Dylan had no doubt that Angelina truly loved her father. Testifying against him, knowing her testimony would probably be the deciding factor between a life sentence and death row, would be the hardest thing she'd ever been asked to do.

Could she do it?

Playacting with the DA was one thing. Sitting in open court in front of a judge, jury and her father would be something else.

He glanced again in the rearview mirror and studied her face. Something was bothering her. She'd been contemplative and quiet all afternoon. And, yes, it had been a tiring and taxing day but Dylan didn't think that was it.

She seemed to be lost in thought. Distracted. Almost as if she had a problem she was trying to solve.

When he could get a few minutes alone with her, maybe after dinner tonight, he'd try and get her to confide in him. He told himself it wasn't that he cared about her feelings and was worried about her. That had nothing to do with it. He was simply doing his job, covering all the angles, being ready and prepared for any occurrence.

He saw her grimace in pain.

Those pills the doctor had given them had helped take the edge off her headaches but her injuries were still too fresh for the pain to be gone. He'd have to re-mind her when they got back to take a couple more be-fore dinner.

As it got closer to rush hour, traffic on the Garden State Parkway was picking up. Not yet congested but getting there. He'd have to keep his eyes more on the road and less on the rearview mirror.

A country-and-western song played on the radio. Donna sang the lyrics and tapped her fingers on her knee to the music. Brad kept trying to engage Ange-lina in conversation but she wasn't having any of it. For some reason, he found that something to smile about.

A glint in the rearview mirror caught his attention. The setting sun had hit the chrome on a motorcycle be-hind him. The biker weaved erratically from one lane to another as if he couldn't decide where he wanted to be. Dylan wondered if the man was driving under the influence.

The traffic on the Garden State Parkway flowed evenly. He didn't note any potential problems. The cars in the fast lane moved at a smooth and steady pace. In his right lane it had been easy to maintain at least two car lengths behind the pickup truck in front of them.

He glanced into his side-view mirror.

The motorcycle, still behind him, maintained its own distance. Seemed the driver had finally picked a lane, the fast lane of course, and was sticking with it.

Dylan relaxed and allowed himself a moment to ad-mire the bike—a Harley-Davidson Road King Clas-sic Screamin' Eagle. He hadn't been on one of those pieces of perfection in years. But once someone rode one of those powerful machines, it wasn't something they soon forgot.

He turned his attention back to the road ahead when he heard the revving of a motor as the biker moved out of the passing lane and pulled even with the bumper of their car.

"Dylan." Brad's tone carried a warning.

"I see him."

Dylan slowed down, hoping this guy was just showing off and would shoot ahead.

He didn't.

Dylan sped up. The bike kept pace.

A warning sensation slithered up Dylan's spine. Something wasn't right. Not by a long shot.

Revving the motor loudly, the biker moved from behind their car and slid up beside Dylan's door.

Donna slipped her gun from her holster and held it on her lap. Dylan knew protocol would have had Brad pull his weapon, as well. A quick glance in the rearview mirror and Brad had already pushed Angelina down on the floor in the backseat.

"Dylan?" Her voice wavered.

"We're fine, Angelina. It's just a precaution. Do as Brad says."

Dylan's muscles tensed as he slowed their car even more.

The biker not only slowed but pulled within inches of the driver's side window. His black helmet and face shield prevented Dylan from seeing the driver's face but he didn't miss the gun in the man's right hand.

"Hang on!" He smashed the accelerator to the floor and the car jolted forward.

Dylan weaved in and out of traffic in a desperate attempt not to hit another car as the speedometer climbed.

Eighty miles per hour. Ninety miles per hour. One hundred miles per hour.

The biker stayed on their tail with ease. Occasionally the driver was able to position himself beside them. That's what worried Dylan the most. He couldn't afford to allow the driver to position his bike for an easy shot.

"He's got a gun!" Dylan warned the other marshals.

Donna removed her seat belt, bent her knees and anchored herself sideways in the seat. She raised her hands and pointed her gun at the cyclist.

"Don't shoot!" Dylan warned. "Not yet. There are too many other drivers. We might hit someone."

Donna agreed but remained ready.

Dylan heard Angelina whimper in the back. "Don't get hurt. Please don't let anybody get hurt."

"Don't worry about us," Dylan commanded. "Just stay down."

"I've got her. Don't worry." Brad released his seat belt and blocked her body with his own.

Faster and faster they flew down the road, the cyclist matching their speed and moves. The speedometer crept to 110 miles per hour. The biker never fired his weapon, never even lifted his hand. It was almost as though he was playing a game of cat and mouse with them, enjoying the chase.

Dylan's worst nightmare loomed ahead. A tractor trailer doing about seventy miles per hour appeared straight ahead. The passing lane held a slow-moving four-door sedan. The white-haired senior citizen at the wheel, who had no business being in the passing lane anyway, putt-putted at about fifty-five miles per hour. Two other cars in both the regular and passing lanes who didn't want anything to do with the racing vchicles they saw in their rearview mirrors quickly pulled over to the shoulder of the road to let them pass. Dylan understood them wanting to get out of the way but now what? They had blocked the shoulder, which was his only avenue of escape, and he had nowhere to go.

The back of that tractor trailer grew with each passing second and Dylan knew if he didn't do something creative and fast, the truck would soon be sitting in their front seat.

Dylan hit the horn again and again never stopping. Then he did the only thing he could do. He straddled the white line and tried to squeeze between the tractor trailer and the senior citizen.

Their car scraped the side of the semi. The screeching sound of metal on metal, horns blasting and brakes squealing filled the air with a cacophony of impending doom. Their sedan bounced off the side of the semi into the passing lane, fishtailed and forced the senior citizen off the road. A quick glance in the mirror showed the car disappearing into the trees and Dylan offered a silent prayer that he hadn't been hurt.

Dylan fought to regain control of their vehicle as they swerved and swayed across the lane. Once he cleared the rig, he pulled in front and gunned it for the nearest exit. Hoping he was in the clear, his stomach tightened when the Screaming Eagle pulled up between the semi and his rear bumper.

"Keep down," Dylan shouted. "He might shoot out the rear window." He swayed in and out of traffic, praying he'd find the opening he needed and that none of the other drivers on the road would be harmed. The bike and its helmeted rider stayed right on his tail.

Just when he thought there could be no other outcome than disaster, he saw that the exit for a wooded rest area was less than a dozen yards ahead. He yanked the wheel a hard right and flew onto the exit. At such a high speed, his back wheels fishtailed back and forth across the road. Sand and gravel shot up, pinging against the metal, the windows, and the front windshield as he tried to bring his vehicle to a halt without hitting anyone or anything.

Dylan didn't need to look in any of his mirrors. The ear-splitting roar of the motorcycle told him it was attached to him like glue. Adrenaline raced through his veins. He slammed on his brakes, almost pushing the pedal into the floorboards and skidded within inches of a tall pine before their car came to a stop.

The motorcyclist roared past them and disappeared onto the highway.

For several seconds, no one moved. No one spoke. Not one word. They simply sat and breathed.

Donna pulled out her cell phone. Her hands visibly shaking, she pressed the numbers on her keypad and called the incident in. Brad holstered his weapon and helped Angelina from the floor to the seat.

It wasn't long before the welcome sound of sirens grew louder with each passing second. The strobe lights from several state trooper cars flashed behind them as they pulled into the rest area.

They were safe. For now.

But that had been close.

Too close.

EIGHT

It was dark when they arrived back in their own neighborhood. Probably eight or later. The street was quiet. The bare limbs on several of the trees looked like skeletal sentinels as their car drove past.

They'd been detained at the site by the troopers for what seemed like hours. Dylan and Brad had fielded most of the troopers' questions. They'd shown their badges but were more tight-lipped with their information than the troopers were happy about and absolutely refused to go anywhere with the men. Calls flew back and forth between the troopers' headquarters and the marshals' office while Angelina and Donna sat in the back of a patrol car and waited for the power struggle between law enforcement to play out.

The final decision was to list Angelina on the reports as a not-to-be-named-or-physically-described witness in an upcoming trial. She was allowed to answer the pertinent questions involving the traffic incident—which was very little since she spent most of her time huddled on the floor of the car with Brad practically sitting on top of her.

She was grateful she hadn't seen much. Between the

day with the DA and now the troopers, she'd had all the questions she could handle.

Although unnecessary, Dylan had also insisted that she be checked out by the EMTs from one of the ambulances called to the scene.

She was fine.

Shaken. Scared. Terrified was more like it. But fine.

No, she couldn't identify the biker.

No, she hadn't seen any of his license plate numbers.

Yes, to the one question no one dared ask. Angelina was certain now that her father knew where she was, who she was with, and was on a mission to stop her. But, of course, she couldn't tell the troopers that nugget of information.

Angelina welcomed the sound of the crunch of tires as they pulled up the gravel driveway. She was exhausted, hungry, spent and grateful to be home if she could call the place that.

She climbed out of the backseat and hadn't taken more than a couple of steps before she sensed Dylan walking directly behind her. She could hear Brad and Donna engaged in a low-volume conversation with each other bringing up the rear.

The porch light came on and the door swung wide. Both Bear and Selma stepped onto the porch.

"Glad to see that everyone is in one piece," Selma said.

Angelina arched an eyebrow. *Selma being concerned? Wow, this really has been a long day.* Then she chided herself for the sarcastic thought. Of course, the woman would be concerned about her colleagues. She'd have to learn to be more charitable.

"We're all right," Dylan answered, moving up to Angelina's side, cupping her elbow and leading her into the house. "Nothing that a little food and a hot shower can't fix."

Bear stepped aside and let them pass. "You don't want me to see that retirement dinner, do you? Trying to give me a heart attack. That's what you're doing."

Dylan chuckled and kept on moving toward the kitchen.

Donna and Brad stepped inside just long enough to gather their things and say goodbye. They were both well past the end of their shift and had to return at 6:00 a.m.

Selma set out plates on the kitchen table. "When I heard what happened and knew you'd be late, I thought you might be hungry when you arrived. I took the liberty to fix something." Donning two oven mitts, she carried a roasting pan to the table and placed it on two heat-insulated pads. Raising the lid, the aroma of pot roast, potatoes, carrots and onions wafted through the room. "But there are plenty of cold cuts and even a few steaks in the freezer if you'd like to fix yourselves something else."

Bear plunked down in the nearest seat and dug right in. "No way. I've been smelling this delight for the past two hours." He spooned a sizable portion onto his plate. "This looks delicious. Didn't know you had it in you, Washington."

Selma hit him with one of her oven mitts. "Why's that, Bear? Just because I am a much more accomplished marksman than you—"

"More accomplished marksman? That'll be the day!"

"—you think I can't find my way around a kitchen? I can multitask, my friend. I didn't see you thinking about pulling anything together for dinner except bologna and cheese sandwiches."

"*More accomplished* and the word *friend* in the same conversation. You do have a leaning toward exaggeration, Washington, don't you?"

"Play nice, people." Dylan held out a chair for Angelina and then moved to the one on her right. Once seated, he leaned forward and cupped her hands in his. "You hanging in there?"

She smiled and nodded.

He straightened, threw an arm over the back of her chair and grinned that bad-boy grin she liked. "It's been quite a day."

Angelina's smile widened into a grin. "That's one word for it." She ladled meat and potatoes onto her plate. "Thanks for this, Selma. It smells wonderful and I am starved."

Could that be a blush tingeing the stern woman's cheeks as she accepted the compliment with a nod?

"So." Angelina caught all the marshals' eyes. "What are we doing for fun, tomorrow?"

Laughter broke out around the table and the rest of the meal passed in a comfortable camaraderie.

Later that night Selma and Angelina retired to bed and Bear and Dylan remained downstairs. Bear leaned against the kitchen counter and looked intently at Dylan. "Want to talk about it?"

Dylan adjusted the brightness on the monitor, studied the vacant backyard for another second, and then looked up and met Bear's gaze.

"Nothing to talk about. Another day at the office."

"Really? That's the way you're gonna play this? With

me? How long we been partners, man?" Bear leaned back, crossed his hands across his gut and waited. "Might as well start spilling. I can wait all night if I have to."

Dylan squirmed beneath Bear's scrutiny. He'd partnered with him long enough to know the man wouldn't let the subject go.

He released a heavy sigh. Maybe it would be good to talk. Venting his feelings might help him understand them a little more. He really wasn't sure he wanted to scrutinize all the muddled thoughts running through his mind and, worse, the messed-up feelings trampling through his heart. But he trusted Bear, always had, always would.

"It was close today, Bear." Dylan turned his head away so his partner couldn't see the flash of emotions on his face.

"Uh-huh." The baritone voice sounded calm and soothing to Dylan's ears. "We've been in close situations before."

"Not ones where I've seen the etchings on our gravestones flash before my eyes."

Bear let out a low whistle. "That bad, huh?"

Dylan pushed back from the monitor and crossed the room to grab a cup of coffee. When he fixed it the way he wanted, he took a sip and turned to face Bear.

Both of them noticed the mug trembled slightly in Dylan's hand. Dylan steadied the mug with both hands and locked his gaze with Bear's. "I almost lost her today. It came down to seconds. A split-second decision this way. A split-second move that way. No time to think. No time to plan. Just survivor mode." Tears burned the back of his eyes and his throat tightened. "It was so close, Bear."

The older man thumped one of his huge hands on Dylan's shoulder. "But you didn't lose her. You kept your head. You got everyone home safe and sound."

"Only by the grace of God."

Bear's teeth shone in a big grin. "Thank God, for the grace of God."

Dylan smiled back and took another mouthful of coffee.

"How did they find you?"

Dylan raised an eyebrow at Bear's question.

"The biker. How did he know where to find you? Did he follow you from the US Attorney's office? And why didn't he finish the job? What made him turn tail and run?"

Dylan shrugged. "You and I both know it's protocol for a witness to be prepared for their courtroom testimony before trial, especially for a trial this big. They've probably been staking out that office all week. We blew it. We should have anticipated the ambush and picked another location or some other means of preparation."

"I hear you on that one. You're right. We dropped the ball." Bear frowned. "What happened to the biker?"

"Don't know. He created a mess, cars everywhere on the Garden State, I suppose he knew the state troopers weren't far behind and took off."

"You said earlier that he had a gun."

Dylan nodded.

"Why didn't he just drive up beside you and shoot you in the head? The resulting crash would have taken all of you out."

"I don't know. I was wondering the same thing myself. He certainly had the opportunity. When I saw the gun in his hand, he was positioned right beside me. It would have only taken a second for him to raise his hand and shoot. But he didn't and I made sure he didn't get a second opportunity."

"That's what I mean, man. It doesn't feel right."

Dylan frowned. "You're thinking that it wasn't a hit."

"You and I have seen mob contracts enforced. They're organized and professional. They do the job quickly, then disappear back into the slime they crawled out from. They don't play tag down a busy freeway and then drive off."

Dylan pondered the information. It made sense. "I'm listening."

"This sounds personal, almost amateurish to me. Playing chicken down the Garden State? If he was trying to take you out, he could have and didn't. So what was he trying to prove? And who was he?"

"You don't think Baroni was behind this, do you?"

"Nope. If he hired a hit man to take you out, I wouldn't be standing here talking to you. You'd be dead and so would everybody else in that car."

"So who? And why?"

"Frankie?"

"Why?" Dylan put his empty mug in the sink, crossed his ankles and his arms, and leaned back against the counter. "If his goal was to kill Maria for breaking up with him, then he achieved it. There's no way he could believe Angelina can identify him. He shot from a position of darkness under the pier. She had her back turned from him and was running away. Even on the off chance he thought she might be able to identify him, this kind of punk runs for the hills. He isn't running. He's showing off like he has something to prove."

"My thoughts exactly." Bear slapped the table with his hand. "This feels like a young punk showing off, like a new rooster in a hen yard strutting around and trying to bring attention to himself, maybe prove a point to someone older."

Dylan's eyes widened. "You think Frankie is trying to prove something to Baroni?"

"That's how it's adding up in my book."

"A power play? Frankie couldn't be that stupid, could he? He's targeting Baroni's daughter? On his own? Without Baroni's order or permission? That's a death sentence!"

"Maybe. Maybe not. Hear me out. The trial starts in four days. Angelina has been missing in action for the past three years but not anymore. She's front and center and ready to testify. What if this young pup decides to kill her before she can testify? Then he plans to go to the big boss and brag about how his actions kept Baroni off death row. He'll be expecting a reward. He'll be expecting to be a 'made man.' He's probably too young, too inexperienced and too low on the totem pole to realize if he pulls a stunt like this, then the capo will have his head. He won't be thanked. He'll be executed for acting on his own without Baroni's permission…and man, to do it to Baroni's *daughter*. This kid is dumber than dirt."

"So you're thinking all the trouble we've been having so far hasn't been coming from Baroni at all?"

Bear shrugged. "Yep. That's exactly what I'm thinking."

Dylan could feel the blood drain from his face. Deep

in his gut he knew Bear was right. The shoot-out in the hospital. The car-bike chase down the Garden State Parkway. Sloppy. Unprofessional. And much too visible. The last thing Baroni would want to do days before his trial would be to draw unnecessary attention to his situation or get any additional law enforcement officials involved.

So they were dealing with a young, rogue, out-of-control hothead. Great!

How were they supposed to stay one step ahead of someone with no logic or self-control?

"If Baroni wasn't behind the last two incidents, he has certainly heard about them by now. With the trial less than four days away, he'll come for her quietly like a thief in the night."

Bear nodded. "Yes, he will."

"How are we supposed to keep her safe, Bear? We have a maverick hothead who is totally unpredictable trying to do the job and then a quiet, professional hit looming around any corner?" Dylan met Bear's eyes and he knew Bear could see the pain and frustration in his expression. "I can't lose her, Bear. Not again."

"I guess this is where I'm supposed to give you the lecture about how we're not supposed to get personally involved with our witnesses."

Anger and embarrassment flooded red in Dylan's face but he couldn't rebuke the truth of Bear's statement.

"Since I'm pretty sure it's too late to do anything about that," Bear continued, "then I suppose we better put our heads together and try to anticipate every possibility and every vulnerable point we may have over the next few days."

"Agreed."

"I suggest we contact the U. S. Attorney's Office first thing tomorrow morning and refuse to take her into his office." Bear gestured to his laptop computer. "We can set up Skype. They can do the remainder of their trial preparation face-to-face right from here."

Dylan nodded. "Good idea. We need to minimize any public exposure."

"Are you sure you weren't followed here?"

"I'm sure. The biker disappeared long before the troopers came and I was diligent on the drive home. No one followed us."

"Good. Then we'll dig in and hibernate for the next few days. We'll have to entertain her so she doesn't go stir-crazy cooped up in the house but that's a small price to pay for safety."

"What if it's not enough, Bear? What if I can't keep her safe?"

"You're doing a good job so far, Dylan. She doesn't have one new scratch on her head from anything that happened to her in our care. That's all we can do. Our best. I'd suggest you have a conversation with the only One who can truly protect any of us. I know I've prayed and I'm not ashamed to say I plan to get on my knees before I turn in tomorrow morning and do it again." He laid his hand on Dylan's shoulder. "Sometimes we can be superheroes and sometimes we are just ordinary men."

NINE

Dylan glanced at his wristwatch. Six forty-five. He finished fastening the buttons on his clean shirt and loped down the stairs, following the delicious aroma of cooked bacon and the sounds of conversation and laughter in the kitchen. When he hit the doorway, he saw Donna, Brad and Angelina gathered at the kitchen table. Bear used a pot holder to lift a black iron skillet from the stove and carried it to a hot pad in the middle of the table.

"Just in time." Bear grinned as he sidestepped Dylan. "I've made a batch of my famous hash brown potatoes with onions and peppers, a slab of bacon, and fresh scrambled eggs topped with butter and cheddar cheese. Fresh pot of coffee over there. You can grab that plate of toast while you're at it."

"Shouldn't you be asleep by now? Your shift ended almost an hour ago."

"I'm gonna get plenty of sleep in just a few minutes. But I sleep better on a full stomach." Bear grinned, showing off those even, white teeth.

Dylan's gaze wandered to Angelina. He'd worried that yesterday's incident would have been a setback for her recovery but he found the opposite. Her bruises were beginning to get the yellowish-purplish tinge of age. Her eyes sparkled with laughter at something Bear had said right before he'd entered the room. They didn't harbor the waves of pain he'd recognized in them the past couple of days. She was getting better and stronger each day.

Now, if he could just keep her that way.

Dylan headed straight to the coffeepot. When he'd filled the largest mug he could find with the welcome brew, he picked up the plate of toast and joined his colleagues at the table.

"Selma get off okay?" he asked.

"She left about a half hour ago," Donna said. "I promised her I'd be right here and ready to leave on time tonight."

Everyone but Dylan chuckled at the lighthearted stab at yesterday's incident.

"Heard we're going to set up a teleconference today instead of going out. Good idea. We get the chance to catch the game," Donna said.

Brad attacked his breakfast as if he'd never eaten before. "Bear, who knew you could cook like this? I'm going to request future details with you if this food service comes with the assignment."

"You think my breakfasts are good? You should see what I can do with a filet of fish. Tell him, Dylan." Bear waved a spatula in his direction. "You went with me to my fishing cabin last summer. I bet the two of us put on five pounds that week just eating my grilled fish and lemon sauce specialty."

Dylan finished a swig of coffee and laughed. "I'll

admit it, Bear. You can cook up a pretty tender piece of fish."

"See! Told ya." The man grinned. "And that's just what this old dog is gonna do on a regular basis six months from now when I can hang up my shield and pull out my fishing pole for good. Ahhh, retirement, here I come."

The sound of laughter was a welcome way to start the day. Dylan just hoped the rest of the day would be as laid-back and happy.

"We'll see how long that lasts, Bear. A couple of months of doing nothing but fishing and you won't even want to see a fishing pole." Dylan finished his breakfast, pushed his plate to the side and pulled his half-full mug front and center. He'd need more than one mug of that brew today. He'd been light on the sleep side lately and it was starting to catch up with him.

"Who said that's all I'm gonna do? I got plans. Lots of plans."

Dylan chuckled again. "Good for you, Bear. But I still think retirement is going to bore you out of your mind."

Bear picked up Dylan's empty plate along with the others. "You're just jealous 'cause you don't know how you're gonna get through a day without me. Ain't easy breaking in new partners, particularly since you aren't going to find anyone as good as me."

Dylan shooed him away. "Yeah, yeah."

"I forgot to tell you," Brad chirped up. "Despite the chaos yesterday, there was one eye witness who had helpful information for the police. He saw two numbers of the license plate of the bike."

Dylan arched a brow. "Really?"

Brad nodded. "I spoke to the boss this morning before shift change. With the detailed description you gave them of the bike combined with the numbers from the witness, they're pretty sure they know who owns the bike that tried to run you off the road."

"Well, are you going to keep us in suspense or are you going to tell us?" Bear grumbled.

Brad grinned. "A guy by the name of Malone. Frankie Malone. Sound familiar?"

Angelina audibly gasped and covered her mouth with her fingers.

"Did they bring him in for questioning?" Dylan asked.

"They haven't located him yet but they will. It's only a matter of time."

Time. The one thing Baroni was quickly running out of.

That evening Dylan perched on the edge of the living room end table and locked his gaze with Angelina's. "You're not still looking for a means to escape, are you? You still intend to testify against your father on Monday?"

"Yes, certainly. I am going to testify."

Those spider-sense alarms scattered across Dylan's nerve endings. Something wasn't right. She was saying all the right things but his gut didn't believe it.

"But?" he prodded.

"No buts."

"Angelina?" Dylan grasped her hand in his. "But?"

"If my father is going to make a move against me, then he has to do it now. He's running out of time."

Dylan nodded and waited for her to continue. Those

sky-blue eyes of hers shimmered with tears and it touched him deeply. All he wanted to do was gather her in his arms and comfort her. But he couldn't. She was a witness. How many times would he have to remind himself?

Still, he found it difficult to look away from her. She was stunning. She wore her emotions on her face, her thoughts behind her gaze, and she, unlike any other woman he'd ever known, had the power to make him *feel*. Really feel. Deep emotions he didn't want to feel or explore.

She is a witness. Only a witness. Your job is to protect her. There should not be any room for feelings. Get your act together. Fast.

Angelina leaned toward him. She squeezed his fingers and her eyes seemed to plead with him to try and understand. Her voice was soft when she spoke.

"People will die, Dylan. People will be killed trying to make sure that I am safe. Your colleagues. Your friends. Maybe even yourself." She stared back hard at him. "I can't let that happen. I'm capable of taking care of myself. You know I am. I've been doing it quite well for the past three years."

She scooted closer, their knees butting. "I don't want to betray you, again. Ever."

He smiled. "Then, don't."

A frantic expression flashed across her face. "You're not listening to me. I need you to help me."

"I am helping you, Angelina. I am keeping you hidden and protected. You're safe with me."

"No! I'm not!" She pulled her hand out of his and brushed a strand of hair out of her eyes. Her fingers trembled. She took a deep breath, exhaled deeply and looked at him again.

"Dylan, please. Help me get out of here. I'll be fine on my own for the weekend. You know I will." She chuckled but it held no humor. "I would probably be safer. But that's not the point. It's not my safety I am worried about. It's everybody else. I can't be responsible for any more deaths. I won't be. Don't you understand?"

Her voice took on an edge of panic. "I don't care what you tell the other marshals. Tell them you and I planned it in advance, and you know where I am and I'm safe. Whatever. But let me slip away. It's not a betrayal, Dylan. I promise you I will be in that courtroom to testify on Monday morning. I just can't sit here any longer and wait for the people around me to be picked off like deer in hunting season."

She reached up and cupped the side of his face, gently, so softly he could barely feel her touch yet it seized his breath.

"It's not a betrayal if I tell you up front." She smiled into his eyes. "So I'm being honest. I'm letting you know I'm going to disappear the very first opportunity I get."

Dylan recoiled as if she'd struck him but recovered quickly. When he did, he was slow to smile, a lazy smile, an indulgent smile. "Well, Ms. Baroni, thanks for the honesty. You've made my job easier." He reached out and tucked that same errant strand of auburn hair that kept popping from beneath her bandage back inside. "I'm not worried about a thing. There is no way on earth that I am going to give you the opportunity.

It's a foolish notion that will only make things uncomfortable and more difficult for all of us."

His smile widened to a grin. "If you really want to help, and I know you do, then help. Do what we ask. Cooperate. Think you can try to do that?"

She sighed deeply and nodded.

He found her stooped shoulders and bowed head strangely reassuring. Maybe she was giving up and accepting the situation. Maybe. He could always hope.

It wasn't long before Selma and Bear rejoined them in the den. Bear suggested a board game. Selma agreed. Dylan begged off. He perched on a stool in the kitchen where he could have one eye on the outdoor cameras via the kitchen monitor and yet have a clear line of view to the three of them in the den.

So she thought she'd slip away, did she? To protect them no less. Her lack of trust in him stung. He wasn't sure whether she mistrusted his federal marshal expertise or if she mistrusted him. Either way, it stung.

Maybe he should try handcuffing her to his left wrist. See what she'd make of that turn of events.

His smile widened. If he tried it, she'd be madder than a hornet whose nest had been knocked over. Feisty. Angry. Coming out swinging. It would almost be worth it just to see the show.

He carefully studied all the camera shots appearing on the monitor. Things were quiet. No activity on the sides of the house. None in the back. They were safe for another night.

But dread cloaked him like a heavy, wet cloth.

Dylan heard that ticking clock in his head. Loud. Foreboding. Relentless. One weekend separating Vincenzo Baroni and a trial that most likely would end with a verdict of lethal injection.

Dylan was sure he wasn't the only one this evening hearing that clock tick away.

TEN

Angelina sat on a chair in front of the large vanity mirror. Her bruises had yellowed and faded. The bandage across her forehead, raggedy and tattered from four days of wear, should be coming off any day now. Selma had mentioned they were taking her to the doctor's office on Monday, after her testimony at the trial, of course.

Angelina cocked her head. She heard Selma moving about in the bedroom. She wasn't a warm and fuzzy companion, that was for sure. But she was diligent about her job, checking the safety of every move not once but twice before enforcing it. Angelina had to admit she felt safe with her...as safe as anyone could when drawing a line in the sand against her father.

She couldn't blame Selma for her constant suspicions. The marshal knew she had run before and expected her to run again. Which, of course, is exactly what she'd been trying without success each day now.

Angelina smiled in spite of herself. She'd checked out the second-story bathroom window. She'd wanted to know how far a drop and if there was anything to break her fall, like maybe a tree branch she could grab hold of as she jumped. But Selma had beaten her to the punch. The window was nailed shut.

Didn't they understand she wasn't trying to run away to get out of testifying against her father? She was determined to testify no matter how difficult it was going to be. Her father had to be stopped.

She was trying to escape to protect *them*.

Over the past few days she'd become fond of Donna and Brad, and, yes, even Selma. She had a special soft spot in her heart for Bear. Who wouldn't? And then there was Dylan.

Her pulse raced and her heart quickened every time she thought about him.

What were her feelings about Dylan?

There wasn't a question in the world that she didn't want him hurt. She didn't want anybody hurt. But with Dylan, her feelings became more complicated.

She still wasn't sure whether she could trust him.

Yes, he had handled their car like a race car driver and saved their lives on the Garden State Parkway. Yes, he had saved her from the shoot-out in the hospital. And, doubly yes, he was attentive and kind and thoughtful despite the fact that three years ago she had played him for the fool.

But…

It was that word *but* that kept her awake at night. She couldn't explain away the note she'd seen pass between Dylan and the bailiff. She couldn't explain away that he'd let someone on her father's payroll within arm's length of her. He couldn't be trusted.

And yet she trusted him, didn't she?

She enjoyed his company. Cared about him. Cared more than she was willing to admit. All the more reason to find a way out. She'd never be able to live with their deaths on her conscience. She had to find a way to escape or die trying. Soon.

"Hey." Selma rapped on the bathroom door. "Are you okay in there? The water stopped running ages ago."

Angelina opened the door. "I'm fine. Daydreaming is all."

Selma nodded, her no-nonsense, professional expression not even cracking a smile at the green goo Angelina had smeared all over her face. "Well, stop daydreaming, come out here, crawl in bed where you belong and try some night dreaming. I heard it's good for you."

Angelina laughed. "Will do. Just let me get this rinsed off." Shortly afterward, she slipped beneath the covers and shut off the bedside lamp. She felt calm, relaxed, more sure of herself than she had been all week.

She watched Selma slide beneath the covers. The woman put on the tiny book light she always carried with her and settled down to read.

Angelina had been paying close attention to Selma for the past couple of nights. The woman read every evening for hours. Every hour or two Selma would stop reading, lean close to Angelina to watch the rhythm of her breathing and try to determine her level of sleep. Only when she was absolutely certain that she was asleep, and knowing the other two marshals manned the house and the cameras, would she allow herself to put down the book and sleep.

That was okay.

Angelina had a pretty good idea of the other men's nightly schedules. She knew Bear stayed in the kitchen on the cameras. Dylan was the only wild card. He didn't have a set schedule. Every few hours she'd see his shadow stretch across the floor beneath the bedroom door. He never knocked. He never undermined Selma's authority. But Angelina knew he was there. Checking. Listening.

Dylan would also spell Bear and it was easy for Angelina to know when he did.

Bear moved around the house like his namesake. He was never quiet. You could hear his large girth stomping through rooms and you always knew where he was.

Angelina had learned to listen to the distant drone of their voices even if she couldn't make out their words. She knew when Dylan was in the kitchen on the cameras. She knew when Bear was resting on the sofa or when he'd grab a newspaper and disappear down the hall to the bathroom.

Dylan would find out soon enough that he wasn't the only one in this house who paid attention to every detail and strategized his next play.

She said good-night to Selma, rolled away from her, closed her eyes and gradually, and as unsuspiciously as possible, slowed her breathing into a normal, slow sleep pattern. Keeping the smile off her face was a more difficult matter.

Sooner or later, Selma would feel safe, let herself fall asleep, and when she did, Angelina would be ready.

Tonight was the last night her presence would keep these marshals in danger.

"Anything?" Dylan nodded his head toward the camera monitor, grabbed a cup of coffee and walked back to stand behind Bear.

"Nada. Nothing. Nil." Bear stifled a yawn. "At this point, I'd be happy to watch leaves fall. Staring at a blank, nonchanging screen for hours is not my idea of fun."

"I'll take nonchanging. No bad guys sneaking around. Sounds good to me." Dylan chuckled and took Bear's seat. "Go ahead and watch some television. I promise the scenes on the television change."

"Want me to go up and check on the girls?"

Dylan couldn't hide the look of horror on his expression.

"What?" Bear asked.

"We want them to sleep, Bear. You clomping up those stairs would wake them." Dylan tried hard but wasn't able to stifle his laugh.

"Very funny. Ha-ha. I'd rather be a he-man and be heard coming rather than a twinkle toes."

"He-man? That's what you call it? How about three hundred ten pounds of solid weight hitting the floorboards?" Dylan laughed harder. "Besides, I checked on the girls before I came in here. All is quiet." He lifted his palm in a halting motion. "Wait. Let me change that assessment. I think I heard Selma snoring."

"Selma, huh? How do you know it wasn't Angelina? Even princesses can snore." Bear crossed his arms, leaned his large frame against the doorjamb and grinned.

Heat rushed into Dylan's face. He wasn't about to tell Bear that three years ago he'd watched Angelina sleep many times before. He'd stand in a doorway and quietly study her face, the way her long eyelashes feathered against her cheeks, the slight parting of her lips. He'd watched her petite form curled up in front of the fire. Firelight shining in her hair. Slumber losing her to another world while he stayed in this one, watching her, protecting her, counting the rhythm of her breathing, fighting with his urge to pick her up and cradle her in his arms.

"Yeah, that's what I thought." Bear chuckled at the beacon of red washing Dylan's face and neck, pushed off from the doorway and headed to the den.

Dylan chased the memories from his thoughts and refused to dwell a moment more in the past. Some doors once closed should remain closed. He didn't know why he found it so hard to do.

At this point in time, he only knew one thing for certain. Angelina didn't snore.

The doorknob twisted easily in her hand. Slowly, and as quietly as possible, Angelina opened the door. When it was ajar enough for her to slip through, she tossed a hurried glance over her shoulder at the bed on the opposite side of the room.

Selma, braced in a sitting position against the headboard, the book light laying askew on the blanket, her book open in her lap, her head lolling to one side, was deeply lost in sleep.

Angelina looked over at her own bed. She had tucked her pillows in such a way that if Selma did awaken a quick glance in the dark might fool the marshal into believing she was still asleep in her bed.

Once she passed into the hallway, she shut the door behind her, flattened her body against the wall, stayed perfectly still and listened. She could hear the deep rumble of the men's voices. Not clear enough to distinguish their words but clear enough to know the men were close together, which meant Bear was still in the kitchen.

Angelina frowned and chewed on her bottom lip. Bear was supposed to be in the den by now. What was the holdup?

Moving as stealthily as possible, she padded in stocking feet down the hallway. Shoes, her jacket and her purse could be retrieved by the front door where she'd left them earlier. The keys to one of the cars would prove to be a bit more of a challenge.

Bear always kept his keys in his pocket, so getting them would be mission impossible. But Dylan often tossed his keys in plain sight. He never seemed to have one location. Sometimes she saw them on the coffee table. Sometimes lying in plain view on the kitchen counter. Once she'd seen them lying on one of the end tables in the den. He wasn't good about keys. Every now and then, he'd hang them on a hook with the jackets by the front door. It was probably too much to hope that tonight would be one of those times, making them easily retrievable. But she could hope.

If the keys weren't there and she didn't see them resting in a place she could get to without detection, then she would have to leave the house on foot. There was a small bathroom, or powder room as they called it, right off the foyer. She'd checked it earlier. The window opened to the bank of bushes on the side of the house, and Selma hadn't thought to nail that window shut.

The carpeting cushioned the sound of her steps as she inched her way down the hallway. Her heart hammered so hard against her chest she thought for sure everyone would be able to hear it beating. Her ragged breathing did nothing to squelch her high level of anxiety.

She could do this. She had to do this. Everyone's

life depended on her putting distance between her father's contract killers and the people in this house who'd sworn to protect her.

She inhaled deeply to try and calm her nerves, which skittered through her body like downed electrical lines in a storm. Her pulse tripped. Her chest constricted. Her stomach clenched. She was a total basket case.

And her head...

The pounding headache she had tonight had nothing to do with a bullet wound or being jostled on her last mob escape and everything to do with fear.

Angelina was scared, bone-deep scared.

So scared her body felt frozen in place and she wasn't sure she could move another inch.

You can do this. You care enough for these people to save them. Do it, now!

She pushed herself forward and was on the third step down the staircase before she paused to listen. She could hear the television on in the den and knew she'd find Bear spread out on the sofa. Rustling and movement in the kitchen followed by a familiar aroma told her Dylan had put on a fresh pot of coffee.

Now or never, girl!

She tiptoed quickly and quietly down three more steps when Dylan's voice made her freeze.

"Bear!"

His feet hit the floor.

"What?" he called, as he moved rapidly toward the kitchen.

Angelina eased down a step. Then, another. Three more steps and she'd be in the foyer and within reach of her personal items and the front door.

"I think we have company." The tension in Dylan's voice gave Angelina pause.

"Where?"

"I'm not sure. It was quick. Too quick. I turned my back to put on a pot of coffee. When I turned around I was sure I caught some movement on the screen."

"Let me see."

Angelina held her breath and counted the seconds, mentally willing the men to finish their conversation. Was someone outside? Had the safe house been compromised?

"I don't see anything." Bear's voice held concern but not alarm. "Maybe it was a cat or raccoon or something."

"Maybe." Dylan didn't sound the slightest bit appeased.

"Want me to go out and take a look?" Bear asked.

"No. You hang here and keep an eye on the monitor. I thought I saw somebody on the side of the garage. I'll slip out the back, go around and check it out."

"Should we wake Selma and have her on standby?"

"Not yet. Give me a minute to check things out. You're probably right about it being a stray cat or small night animal. I didn't get a good look, only caught movement, not object or size. I never should have taken my eyes off the screen."

"Hey, knock it off. You made a pot of coffee. Big deal."

"Let's hope it's not a big deal. Let's hope it's nothing at all."

Angelina heard the rustling sound of Dylan slipping into his jacket and was thankful he'd had it in the kitchen with him and not hanging on a hook in the foyer.

"I'll come back in the same way I'm going out. Keep an eye on me on the monitor. If you see anything strange, anything at all, phone Selma's cell and wake her up. Then call 9-1-1, and don't let me back through that door for any reason unless I give you the agreed upon password. Understood?"

"Got it."

This was her chance. Bear would be tied to the monitors. Dylan would be outside and moving to the left side of the house near the garage. If she wanted to run, it was now or never.

She raced down the last three steps, threw on her shoes, and grabbed her jacket and purse from the hook beside the door. She reached for the doorknob but pulled back instantly before she could open it. The doorknob had burned her palm. She glanced at her hand unsure of what just happened.

When she recovered from her shock, she ran to the window and pushed back a curtain.

Oh no! Oh, dear Lord, please help us!

Angelina raced into the kitchen. "Wait!"

Bear was just sitting down at the monitor, stopped in midmotion and looked back at her.

Dylan paused in the open doorway to the backyard, a deep burrowed frown on his forehead as he stared at her. "Angelina?"

"The house." She cupped the palm of her right hand with her left and looked with surprise at the blisters already forming on it. Fear pummeled at her heart and threatened to steal her voice but she wouldn't let fear win. "It's on fire!"

ELEVEN

Bear sprang into action. He grabbed the fire extinguisher from beneath the kitchen sink and turned in her direction. "Where?"

Dylan slammed the back door and rushed back into the kitchen.

"There." With hands shaking so badly she could hardly aim straight, Angelina pointed at the monitor.

Both men swiveled their heads in the direction she'd pointed.

The three of them watched in stunned silence as flames engulfed the bushes in front of the house, climbed the vinyl siding, and rapidly spread along the sides of their building.

Dylan stared hard at the monitor.

"How could this be, Bear? No fire could start this easily and spread this fast. Unless…"

Multiple men dressed in black appeared on different camera angles on the screen. They doused the house with a liquid accelerant. Other shadows stepped out of the gloom on the other side of the house and within seconds fire surrounded the home. The sound of shattered glass and thuds hit the roof.

"They're hitting the roof with Molotov cocktails," Bear yelled.

Their adversaries continued to douse liquid on the already burning material and the flames shot higher turning the house into a tinderbox.

Bear grabbed his cell phone and instantly dialed Selma.

"She won't hear you," Angelina said, her voice filled with panic. "I threw her phone in the toilet."

Bear looked at her incredulously. "You did what?" He took off at a run calling Selma's name on each step as he raced upstairs.

Angelina put her hands against her face. "I'm sorry, Dylan. I had no idea something like this was going to happen. I…"

Dylan's face resembled a carved granite mask. He grabbed her right wrist, clamped one end of a pair of handcuffs to it, and put the other end on his own left wrist.

"Dylan, I—"

"Don't!" His tone brooked no argument. "Don't even try to explain. We don't have time to listen to anything you have to say. I know exactly what you thought you were doing. If you have one ounce of conscience left in your body, you'll do as we tell you to do and help us get out of this mess."

She nodded and lowered her arm to her side. She didn't mutter a word of protest or make a sound. The tight, heavy metal bit into her wrist as Dylan moved about the room with her in tow yet she offered no complaint.

He called 9-1-1 and reported the fire. He speed dialed his boss and called for backup. He ran to the bottom of the steps just in time to see Selma and Bear racing down.

The smoke that had been seeping beneath the front door rose toward the ceiling and a thick, gray fog formed throughout the house, making it almost impossible to see more than a couple of feet inside the rooms. Flames consumed the door panels and spread through the drywall in the foyer. The acrid smell of smoke scorched their throats and intense heat seared their faces. Fingers of fire crept across the carpeted floor and quickly ignited the draperies and furniture.

Bear drew his weapon, pointed it toward the ceiling and continued down to the bottom stair. Selma followed suit.

"Where are they?" Bear asked.

"Do you know how many?" Selma asked. "Did you recognize anybody?"

"I counted four," Dylan shouted, also removing his weapon. "But there could be more. I didn't wait around to see."

A Molotov cocktail flew through the front plateglass window and within seconds the entire living room was a wall of flame.

The four of them, choking and coughing as smoke filled their lungs, crouched low and ran to the kitchen. No sooner had they reached the kitchen when a second Molotov cocktail sailed through the window over the sink almost smashing into Bear.

He jumped backward. "We've got to get out of here." He straightened to lead the way through the smoke to the back door when a bullet slammed into his right shoulder and he dropped his weapon. Scrambling to retrieve it, he pointed the gun with his left hand and aimed out the window in the direction of the gunfire and fired his weapon. A second bullet found a home in his abdomen.

A hail of bullets flew into the kitchen, thudding into cabinets, countertops and doors.

Bear and Selma dropped to a crouch behind the island counter. Selma drew her weapon and returned fire.

Dylan shoved Angelina to the floor next to them. "Stay down," he warned.

Bullets continued to pierce cabinets and walls. The three marshals returned gunfire.

Dylan shielded her body with his own. He raised his head and glanced at the monitor.

"I see three, no four in the backyard, and they're wearing night goggles."

Bear sprang up, fired, then crouched back down.

Selma lifted the edges of Bear's shirt. "Let me see." She glanced at the wound. "You'll live but try not to get another one."

"Thanks, but I wasn't trying to get the first one."

Angelina's eyes burned and watered making it difficult for her to see a thing. The crackling sounds of fire roared in her ears. Her throat constricted from breathing in the thick black smoke that was quickly filling the kitchen. She coughed uncontrollably, each cough making it harder to draw in a good breath.

"We've got to get out of here," Selma said. She tucked a dish towel inside Bear's shirt against his stomach wound to try and stanch the flow of blood.

"If they've got men in the back of the house, they'll have them in the front, too," Dylan said. "We'll be spotted the second we try to open any of the doors." He jumped up, yanked open the nearest drawer and grabbed some more dish towels. Keeping his head low so as not to get shot, he drenched them in the nearby sink and tossed two of them to his colleagues.

Crouching back down, he turned to Angelina. "Put this over your nose and mouth. It should help." He aided her tying the towel behind her head and then tied his own.

"Take Angelina through the garage. Selma and I will try to draw their attention and give you a chance to get out of here." Bear crawled toward the back door. "I'll take the back. Selma, grab a broom, open the front door with it. Keep out of the line of fire."

"Bear, you won't stand a chance," Dylan said. "They have night vision. You'll be a sitting duck."

Bear gestured to the flames that were quickly engulfing the house. "We're already sitting ducks. We've got to split up. Now move."

Gasping for air, despite the wet cloth over her mouth and nose, Angelina followed Dylan's lead. They made their way to the garage and slipped inside. The cinder block walls had kept the flames at bay. Both of them lowered their towels and pulled clean, fresh air into their lungs.

Dylan put his face close to hers. "Are you all right?" She nodded.

"We have one chance to get out of here and it's a slim one."

Angelina tried not to let her terror show on her face.

"We can't afford to wait for help to get here. We're going to have to try and shoot our way out of the garage and make a run for it."

Angelina nodded. "Okay. Just tell me what to do."

The fact that her teeth didn't chatter when she spoke surprised her. She'd never been more scared in her life.

The sound of gunfire blasted from both the front and back of the house.

Bear and Selma had made their moves.

"Now!" Dylan yelled. He hit the garage door opener, moved to the front, and as soon as there was enough space, he squirmed beneath it pulling Angelina with him and firing his weapon with his free hand every inch of the way.

Bullets hit the graveled drive beside Angelina spraying her body with small bits of rock that imbedded in her flesh. The handcuff biting deeply into her skin left a raw and painful ring but she didn't dare complain. She'd brought it on herself. Besides, she knew it wasn't punishment. Dylan didn't want to lose her in the chaos.

Within seconds, Dylan was on his feet again, dragging her with him, firing into the darkness.

Sirens sounded in the distance and Angelina looked hopefully in that direction.

A bullet whizzed past her ear. She buried her head in the back of Dylan's arm and they crouched behind one of the cars parked in the driveway. Help was on its way.

But would it get there in time?

Bear appeared out of nowhere. Bleeding from his head, his chest and his gut, he sank down beside them. "I got two of them. Winged a third. The fourth one got away."

"Selma?"

"I don't know. I saw her crumbled in a heap on the front step. I couldn't get to her to check her out."

Dylan removed his jacket, rolled it in a ball and

shoved it on top of the soaked-through dish towel inside Bear's shirt. He applied pressure trying to stanch the continued flow of blood. "Here, press down hard. Help will be here any minute."

"Are they gone?" Angelina whispered. "I don't hear anybody shooting anymore."

"Yeah, I think so. They heard the sirens and took off running."

A bullet crashed into the metal beside Bear's head and he ducked. "Well, most of them did. I guess Malone decided to finish the job."

"Malone?" Dylan sprang up, returned fire and ducked down again. "Are you sure it's Malone?"

"I'm sure." Bear coughed, moaning in pain and grabbing his abdomen. "Got to see him up close and personal when he did this to me."

More bullets flew their way.

"Keep down," Dylan ordered, pushing Angelina down with one hand and returning fire with the other.

A sickening thud followed by the sound of a "humph" drew Angelina's immediate attention. She recognized that sound. She'd heard it on an Atlantic City beach when her best friend, Maria, had been fatally hit.

"Dylan!" She caught him as he collapsed against her lap. A pool of blood appeared on the left side of his shirt and Angelina experienced a painful déjà vu. Her mind flashed a similar sight of the stain on the front of Maria's dress moments before she'd collapsed dead at her feet.

"Dylan!" Tears streamed in an unstoppable flow down her face. "Don't you die!" She grabbed the shirt material in her hands. "Don't you dare die on me."

Bear's body shook with one cough after another but

he managed to crawl over to Dylan's side. He slapped his face. "Hey, whatcha doing? Open those eyes. We need a superhero right now and that ain't me." He coughed again.

Dylan opened his eyes.

Angelina threw one arm around him and sobbed.

Dylan tried to sit up. "I'm okay." He looked at the blood seeping through the left side of his chest. "Just a flesh wound."

The sirens grew louder.

Angelina's body racked with sobs as she mentally urged the paramedics and firefighters closer.

Bear fumbled in his pocket, took out a set of keys and pressed them into Dylan's hands. "Get her out of here."

"What?" Angelina looked at him in shock. "We're not going anywhere. Help is coming. Can't you hear the sirens?"

Bear clamped one of his beefy hands on Dylan's arm. "It was an inside job. We have a mole. No way Malone found our safe house on his own."

Dylan acknowledged his statement with a nod.

"Get her out of here. It's your last chance, man. Take her to my fishing cabin. No one knows where it is but us. You'll be safe."

Dylan's eyes widened at the sight of the blood drenching through the jacket he had pressed against Bear's abdomen. Pressure hadn't stopped the flow. "I'm not leaving you," he said.

Bear squeezed Dylan's forearm hard. "Yes, you are. I'm not dying for nothing. Get out of Dodge. Keep her safe. Bring her to trial on Monday."

"You're not going to die." Unshed tears scorched the

back of Dylan's eyes and seized his throat. "I refuse to let you die."

Bear's attempt at a laugh ended in a spasm of coughs. When he could speak, he whispered, "You don't make those decisions. Now get out of here. Keep her safe."

Dylan glanced at Angelina. She shook her head. "No, Dylan. You're injured, too. We have to wait for help."

He ignored the pleading in her eyes. He ignored the excruciating pain in the vicinity of his heart when Bear's eyes rolled back and finally closed. Not knowing or caring whether the pain in his chest was his own bullet wound or the sight of the broken and bleeding body of his partner didn't matter. It was excruciating and momentarily paralyzing.

But he reminded himself he was a US federal marshal.

He needed his training to kick in. He needed his body to operate on autopilot and listen to his mind and not his heart. Bear was right. Nothing was going to stop him from protecting his witness. With a heavy heart and renewed determination, he yanked his left wrist, pulling Angelina to her feet.

"We're getting out of here. Now!"

Amid a hail of bullets, they ran.

TWELVE

Moving with stealth and speed, Dylan opened the passenger door of his car and climbed inside. "Climb over me," he ordered. "You've got to drive."

He pulled her into the car. "Stay as low as you can. Don't be an easy target," he ordered.

Angelina hurried to do as he requested, banging her head on the ceiling as she scrambled over Dylan and jarring her thigh on the shift stick between the seats.

No one fired at them. That was a good sign, right?

She settled into the driver's seat, took the keys from Dylan and shoved them into the ignition. A quick glance his way spiked an adrenaline rush that pulsed through her body. His eyes were closed. His head hung toward his left shoulder. His wet shirt clung to his chest and for a second she was afraid he was gone.

She stared in horror at his chest, not realizing she was holding her breath until she heard the slight rise and fall of his own.

The wail of sirens drawing closer made her hopes grow.

"Dylan." She reached over and shook his arm. "They're only seconds away. We should wait. You need help."

"Drive!"

"But…"

He reached over and turned the key. "For once in your life listen to me. Drive!"

Angelina threw the car in Reverse and hit the accelerator. Their tires squealed and threw up gravel as she pulled out into the street. Their neighbors, drawn by the fire and the commotion, huddled on the opposite curb.

"Where are we going?"

"Get out of this neighborhood as quickly as you can. Do you know how to get to the Garden State Parkway from here?"

Angelina nodded.

"Do it."

Dylan turned away, watching out the passenger side-view mirror to see if anyone tried to follow them. He placed his drawn weapon on his leg.

The reflection of flashing red lights beamed off the rearview mirror. The first fire truck pulled up to the curb. A police car and second fire engine pulling in right behind it.

A knot the size of a boulder settled in Angelina's stomach.

Help was there—right there, right now—and she was driving away.

With a heavy sigh and heavier heart, she pushed her foot harder on the accelerator and sped in the opposite direction down the street.

About forty-five minutes later and heading north, Angelina spoke for the first time since they'd left the scene.

"Do you think we're being followed?"

"No. I haven't seen anything suspicious. I think Frankie took off when he heard the sirens."

Sweat beaded on Dylan's forehead. Deep lines etched the sides of his mouth as he grimaced in pain. His breathing appeared shallow and labored.

"Dylan, you need help."

"I'll be fine. We have to make it to the cabin. That's all I care about right now."

"But you're hurt. And it doesn't look like the bleeding has stopped."

He glared at her.

She felt like Daniel in the lion's den and held her breath waiting for an attack. Mustering what little courage she could find, she said, "What happens if you pass out? Or worse, die? What am I supposed to do then?"

"I'm not going to pass out." His eyes held a determination she'd never seen before and an intense anger.

She shot him a puzzled look. "Why are you so angry with me?"

"What were you doing in that foyer with your coat and shoes on, Angelina? If the fire hadn't stopped you, what would you have done?"

She turned her head and looked back at the road.

"Dylan, you don't understand. It wasn't a betrayal. I was trying to save everyone from exactly what has happened tonight. But I was too late."

"Drive," he snapped at her. "Just drive."

She drove a few more minutes in silence before daring to speak again. "Where are we going? You never told me where Bear's cabin is."

A flash of pain crossed Dylan's expression at the mention of his partner's name. "It's up in Bear Mountain."

"Bear Mountain? New York? We're crossing state lines?"

"You have a problem with that?"

She shook her head but her heart sank into her stomach. Once they left New Jersey jurisdiction her hopes of the local police finding them and helping them would be quickly dashed.

"I saw an ambulance pull up behind one of the fire trucks," Angelina offered. "I'm sure Bear's in good hands."

Dylan's expression darkened. He remained silent.

"I couldn't see Selma. Did you?"

More silence.

"Dylan, I really think we should go back. You need medical care. The police and the marshals will be able to protect us better than the two of us on the run alone, injured, almost unarmed—you can't possibly have much ammunition left in that gun."

The hostile look Dylan shot her sent a shiver of goose bumps down her spine.

"Now you trust the police and the marshals?" He glared at her. "Do me a favor, okay? Stop talking. Stop trying to justify what you almost did tonight. I can't trust you, Angelina. And I have too much on my mind to worry about it now. Let's just get to safety."

Dylan spent the next few minutes giving her directions to the cabin.

Angelina had a heavy heart. Dylan was hurt both physically and emotionally and she felt responsible for all of it. Knowing there was nothing else she could say, she turned her attention to the road. They still had a long drive ahead of them.

The remainder of the trip passed in a heavy, strained silence.

* * *

The bumping of the car along an uneven surface and the sound of tires hitting small scattered branches and gravel on the dirt road stirred Dylan from slumber. He raised his head and looked through the windshield.

"Where are we?" It took him a moment to get his bearings.

Angelina pulled the car to a stop. Headlights illuminated a small front porch with two straight back chairs attached to a small wooden cabin.

"Is this it?" Angelina looked over at him. "Am I at the right place?"

Dylan relaxed. "Yes. You followed my directions perfectly." He looked her way. "I'm sorry I drifted off. Why didn't you wake me?"

"I wasn't sure if you were sleeping or unconscious and I was too afraid to find out."

A wave of guilt washed over him. He'd been harder than necessary on her and, yet, she'd stayed on task and gotten them to safety. "You did a great job. Thanks."

She nodded but remained silent.

Dawn claimed the horizon. They'd been driving for hours and were both exhausted.

"Are you sure no one followed us?" he asked.

"Not unless they've been driving for the past thirty miles without headlights. I haven't seen signs of anyone or anything ever since we left the main roads."

"Good."

Angelina jiggled her right hand. "Think maybe you could take this cuff off now?"

With a sober expression, Dylan shook his head. "I'm sorry. I just can't take the chance."

Defiance flashed across her face and then was gone.

"Right. I'm going to take off on foot and walk through the woods on a mountain with no food, no water and no weapon. Sure I am."

She sighed heavily and looked intently into his eyes. "You're hurt. I am not going to take off and leave you when you're injured."

Dylan wanted to believe her. He needed to believe her. But she'd lied to him before and he couldn't afford to let it happen again. After all, she'd been warning him for days that she was looking for the first opportunity to take off and he was determined not to give it to her.

"We'll talk about it later. For now, climb over me. Let's go inside and get settled. I'm sure you're as exhausted as I am."

She knew he didn't trust her. The saddened look in her eyes was almost his undoing. But rather than protest or try to fight him, she simply handed him the car keys and did as he asked.

She moved as quickly and gently as possible crawling across him and seeming to do her best not to jostle or touch his wound. Still it hurt. Pain seized his chest and made him catch his breath.

She helped him out of the car.

He couldn't throw his left arm over her shoulder for support due to the handcuffs but, still, he couldn't take the chance to remove them. He leaned his left arm heavily against her. She seemed to understand and leaned just as heavily against him, giving him the support he needed to climb the three steps to the porch. He fumbled with the keys to unlock the door.

Angelina took the keys from his hand, unlocked the door and as best as she could encumbered with cuffs, helped him inside.

Dylan collapsed into the nearest chair, pulling Angelina into a seated position on the floor beside him.

Her mouth twisted in frustration. "For a smart man this is the stupidest thing you can do." Anger laced her words. "I can't sit on the floor for two days. I need to be able to walk around the room. Use the bathroom. Sleep in a bed." She jiggled the cuffs. "I can't take a look at your wound and help you get cleaned up if I'm chained to your side like an animal."

A gamut of emotions tumbled inside his aching head. He knew she was right. He couldn't keep her cuffed to him. But how could he trust her after what she had done before?

It was almost as if she could read his mind. Gently she reached up and cupped the side of his face in her palm. "I understand, Dylan. I do. I betrayed you once before. You're afraid that I'm going to do it again, especially since I told you I was going to try and get away and then did try. I would have been successful, too, if it hadn't been for the fire."

A bittersweet smile laced her mouth and she pulled back her hand. She gazed at him intently, a deep sadness in the depths of her eyes. "But there's no reason for me to run now. It's too late. All I wanted to do was to protect you and the other marshals. The worst has already happened." A tear slid down her cheek. "I'm so sorry, Dylan, about Bear and Selma." She took a deep breath. "But you have to trust me. It's just us. We have two days left before we have to be in Camden at the Federal Courthouse for the trial. We need to work together. We need to help each other." She moved closer to him, placing her hand on his leg. "Please. Try to trust me. You're injured. Let me help you. I promise I will not leave you."

His heart ached at the sound of her words, at the look in her eyes. He was exhausted, in pain, grieving the loss of his best friend. His jumbled thoughts mixed with his emotions. He wasn't sure any decision he made right now would be the correct one.

But what choice did he have?

He needed help. He needed his wound cleaned, the bullet probably dug out. He knew he was fighting with all his might to stay conscious but had already nodded off in the car. If he fell unconscious, or worse, died, he couldn't have her chained to him. He fished the handcuff key out of his right pocket and released the cuffs.

"Please, Angelina, don't make me regret this." He watched as she pulled her hand back and rubbed her wrist. It looked raw and sore and he felt a pang of guilt.

"Thank you."

He nodded. His chest hurt so much he almost couldn't feel the pain anymore. His head spun. A dark curtain filled his peripheral vision and his stomach roiled. Was this what it felt like to be on the brink of death? What was going to happen to Angelina if he couldn't hold on?

She leaned closer to him. Wetness welled in her eyes. She kept her voice soft and soothing. "I'm going to look at your wound. I don't have any medical training but I am going to try and help you."

They were the last words he remembered hearing before he lost his battle with the blackness that chased him.

"Dylan." She shook his arm. Unable to rouse him, she put her fingers on his throat to feel for a pulse. She almost cried with joy when she found one. She opened the buttons on his shirt. Blood had dried around the far edges of the wound, sealing the material to his skin, but fresh liquid seeped from the center against her fingertips.

How much blood had he lost? How much more could he afford to lose? If she tried to pull the shirt away from the dried blood on his skin, would it reopen the wound? But she had no choice. She couldn't help if she couldn't see how badly he'd been wounded.

First, she needed supplies.

Angelina stepped back from Dylan's chair and took a few precious minutes to familiarize herself with the cabin. Not unexpectedly, Bear had shut off the electricity in his absence. Thankfully, it was almost dawn and enough light seeped into the cabin, making it possible for her to see.

Her eyes swept the room. The cabin lacked a woman's touch. It was utilitarian, stark and screamed "man cave" in every direction from mismatched furniture, fish mounted on plaques on the walls, an unadorned stone fireplace in the center of the room, fishing gear mounted on the right wall and a gun rack on the left one.

She found gauze bandages in the bathroom cabinet and a fully stocked first aid kit including a suture kit. She even found a men's grooming kit with tweezers that she could use if she had to dig out the bullet in his chest. Just the thought that she might have to do that turned her stomach and her hands shook.

She finished searching the bathroom cabinet and vanity. Knowing she couldn't delay any longer she did something she didn't think she would ever do again but found she was doing with regularity these past few days—she bowed her head and prayed.

She offered a prayer of gratitude that they were still alive and had reached the safety of the cabin. She told the Lord how sorry she was for having been so distant, like a spoiled brat who wanted to control her life rather than give that authority to the only One capable of controlling life. Then, she prayed that if it was His will, that He give her the strength and the skill where skill didn't exist to help Dylan.

Please, Lord. Please spare his life. All he is doing is trying to spare mine.

An inner peace filled her being. Whatever the future held, Angelina knew they would not be facing it alone and tears streamed down her face. She had come home.

She gathered clean towels and a basin of soapy water and hurried to Dylan's side. Gently, she pulled away the material so she could examine the wound. The dried edges of the wound did reopen but quickly clotted. It was the main body of the wound that troubled her.

Angelina took scissors and cut the front of his shirt away to get a better look. She gasped when she saw the gaping hole in his chest staring back at her. Was the bullet still in there? Hoping it had passed through his body, she gently slid her left arm behind his back and leaned him forward, supporting his upper body against her right arm so she could see if there was an exit wound.

Be there. Please, please be there.

She couldn't believe she was actually hoping to find a second open wound. But there wasn't one.

The bullet hole was located on the far left wall of his chest beneath his collarbone and closest to his arm. Thankfully it was far enough from his heart that she believed it hadn't hit any major organs or done any permanent damage. Now if she didn't botch things trying to dig the bullet out, Dylan might be okay.

A moan escaped his lips when she lowered him back against the chair. His eyelids fluttered and then he opened his eyes. He appeared dazed for a minute or two, as if he was trying to clear his head. He took notice of the supplies on the table beside him and seemed to understand where he was and what was happening.

"Did the bullet pass through?" He forced the words out through teeth gritted in pain.

"No."

He released a deep sigh. His tone of voice held resignation and determination. "Dig it out."

Angelina's hands began to tremble. "I…I don't know if I can. It would have been easier if you were still unconscious but I can't do it while you're awake, while you can feel…" Tears flowed freely.

Dylan captured one of her hands in his. "You need to do this." He squeezed his eyes shut. When he opened them again he released her hand and tilted her chin until their gazes locked. "You will be saving my life, Angelina. No matter how much I moan or cry out please keep reminding yourself that you are saving my life."

Dylan looked over the supplies lying on the end table. He saw the bandages, antiseptic, suture kit, tweezers. "You need a knife." He looked back at her. "There are some filet knives that Bear used to skin fish. They are thin, sharp and should do the job." He glanced around the dimly lit cabin. "We don't have fire to sterilize anything with but I believe there is rubbing alcohol in the bathroom."

Angelina lifted a bottle of alcohol from the floor beside her.

"Good. You thought of that already." He grinned and, even though it looked like a forced grin, it did its job and made her relax a bit. "See," he said. "You're going to do a fine job."

He watched her douse the knife and the tweezers in alcohol. "Good. Hand me one of those flashlights."

She did.

He turned it on and held it in place high on the right side of his chest.

"We want you to be able to see what you're doing." Another forced grin, but Angelina deeply appreciated that he was more concerned with her emotional comfort than his physical one. "Now fold a dishcloth in thirds and put it between my teeth."

Angelina's eyes widened and fear crept up her spine again.

His eyes bore into her. "You can do this. You can. Tune me out. If I moan or cry out, don't stop. Don't stop for anything no matter what. Understand? Just keep telling yourself that you are saving my life because you are."

"Pray with me."

His eyes registered surprise since she'd been adamant in the past that she no longer prayed, but a glint of happiness that she wanted to pray lit his eyes. Together, they bowed their heads in prayer.

When they had finished, Angelina put the towel between his teeth and picked up the knife.

As she probed the wound to get close to the edge of the bullet, her admiration for Dylan increased tenfold. He stared at the ceiling, staying as still as possible and did his best not to make a sound. It was the beaded sweat on his forehead and how tightly his teeth clenched down on the towel that told her how much pain he was in. She almost cheered when she finally saw the round rim of the bullet and knew his ordeal was almost over.

"I've found it."

Dylan blinked hard and nodded encouragement.

Angelina took the tweezers, worked a little longer, a little harder and was finally able to pull the bullet out. She sat back on her legs and breathed a heavy sigh of relief.

She dipped a clean cloth into a bowl of clear water and gently washed the sweat from Dylan's brow. He drew his mouth into a grim line. Pain radiated from his eyes. Still, he remained calm and quiet.

"We're not out of the woods, yet." Her fingers traced down his face in an effort to offer comfort. "The wound appears deeper and wider than I'd like. I'm afraid it won't close on its own. I'm going to have to try and stitch it closed in order to stop the bleeding."

Dylan nodded and spat the material out of his mouth. "Do what you have to do."

"I'm not a doctor. I haven't ever stitched anyone up before. You're going to have a terrible scar."

Dylan laughed unexpectedly. "I'll live with the scar, Angelina." His eyes sobered. "Thanks to you, I'll live, period." He smiled. "Go for it. Just don't embroider flowers or smiley faces into my chest."

Angelina laughed, too, and the tension in the room melted away. When she finished, she cleaned the wound, lathered it with antiseptic cream, and covered it with gauze and cloth strips to hold it in place. When she raised her eyes, she noted caked blood in Dylan's hair just above his temple. Upon close examination, she realized that another bullet had grazed his skull. A sick feeling rushed through her.

She cleaned that wound, too. Holding the bandage in place by wrapping a few rows of gauze around his forehead, she couldn't help but touch her own bandage and grin.

"Look, Dylan. We're a match." She allowed herself to laugh at the irony of it all.

His eyes caught hers and a sudden intimacy filled the room. The intensity of his stare captured her breath.

"I agree," he said, a husky undercurrent in his voice. "We are a perfect match, aren't we?"

THIRTEEN

Angelina didn't answer, not sure whether to take his words at face value or examine their meaning. An awareness, almost a palpable electricity, connected them. When he continued to stare at her, heat flooded her face and pulsed through her veins. Not knowing what to do with all those jumbled and confused feelings inside, she pushed away from his chair and acted as if nothing powerful, nothing potentially life-changing, had just occurred between them.

Not able to meet his eyes, she busied herself gathering the supplies.

"Try and rest while I clean up the mess I made. I don't think I've seen you sleep more than an hour or two in the past forty-eight hours. You're going to need your strength."

With her arms wrapped around the basin of water, she forced a smile on her face and dared to glance in his direction.

His eyes spoke volumes. He knew she was avoiding the issue, avoiding the talk that inevitably they would have to have. But his shoulders relaxed and she knew that he was willing to let it go for now.

"Thanks again. I owe you." Even though pain etched deep furrows in his brow and clouded his eyes, he smiled at her.

"You don't owe me anything. Not too many people get the opportunity to carve their initials into a federal marshal's chest."

The feigned look of horror on his face made both of them laugh and the atmosphere in the room returned to normal, whatever normal between them was.

"Can I get you anything? Are you hungry?" she asked.

"A glass of water would be appreciated."

"Coming up." She made it back and forth from the kitchen in record time. She handed him water along with the two pain pills she'd taken out of the first aid kit. "I know these won't be much help with the pain but they might take the edge off."

She watched him grimace with even the slightest movement but he accepted the pills from her hand and swallowed them.

"Dylan, why don't you go in the bedroom and lie down? You need the rest and it will be more comfortable than sitting in that chair."

"I'm staying here."

"Why? That's foolish."

"It's foolish to guard the only entrance and exit to the building? Don't think so. If I stay here, I can see anyone approaching." He shot her a telling glance. "And I can stop anyone from leaving."

She shook her head. "You are a stubborn man. If I wanted to leave, I could have left hours ago while you were sleeping."

"You probably stayed because you didn't know where we are or how to get out of here."

"Yeah, right. Who do you think drove us here in the first place? And even if I did forget, haven't you ever heard of GPS?" She crossed her arms and stared him down. "I stayed because I didn't know if you were going to live or die. For some stupid reason, I didn't want you to die."

She saw him try to stifle a smile and the thought he was laughing at her grated on her nerves. Stomping her foot in frustration she stormed off into one of the bedrooms. The man had an incredible ability to get under her skin one way or the other and none of the ways bored her that's for sure. Okay, so she pulled a doozy three years ago. And, yes, she was trying to take off again last night. But she'd explained why. And the circumstances now were entirely different. Why didn't he trust her? And more baffling why did it bother her so much that he didn't?

After taking a few minutes to get her temper under control, she retrieved a blanket from the bed, dragged it into the main room and placed it over him. "If you're going to insist on playing big brave caveman and guarding our cave, then you need to try and rest. That wound was nasty. I did the best I could with it but I'm sure it hurts."

He nodded. "It does but I can handle it."

She gave an exasperated sigh. "Fine. Handle it. But try to get some rest, too." She clasped her hands in a begging motion. "Please. Do it for me. When we get back to civilization it would be nice if you were alive and well and I could show off my wound-care skills."

He offered her the briefest of smiles. "Okay, just for

you." His eyes looked so heavy Angelina didn't think he'd have much choice in the matter, anyway.

"I think I will close my eyes but just for a minute." He rested his head against the back of the chair.

Angelina watched him in silence. When she was certain he was as comfortable as she could make him, she set to work. She emptied the basin she had set aside in the kitchen. Put the first aid kit back on the shelf in the bathroom. Then, hurried back to Dylan's side.

A light snore escaped his lips and her smile widened. *Yep, you go ahead and snore.*

It was the best sound she'd heard in the past twenty-four hours. Being careful not to wake him, she tucked the blanket in around him to ward off the October morning chill. Then, she brought in firewood already stacked on the front porch and set to work building a fire.

Fire.

Wasn't it amazing that the same object when controlled in a fireplace could offer such comfort and when uncontrolled could cause such chaos and loss?

The warmth of the flames heated her skin and seeped into her bones.

Satisfied with her efforts, she relaxed for the first time since the string of events started the night before. She wasn't a doctor but had done a reasonable job tending to Dylan's wounds. She'd never been a girl scout but had started a decent fire in the fireplace. She allowed herself a moment of self-satisfaction. She knew God had guided her hands and she offered a silent prayer of thanks.

Although her position in front of the fire left her toasty warm and comfortable, she didn't allow herself to stop. Not yet. She searched the cabinets for food. Although there was nothing in the refrigerator since the electric was off, she found canned soup she could heat up later for dinner. She also found some dry cereal they could munch on, a variety of canned vegetables and a couple cans of tuna fish. She rummaged a little more and found instant coffee, packets of sugar and even a small container of whole milk that didn't need refrigeration until opened. Maybe if she put it outside after she opened it the weather would keep it fresh enough to use for the next two days.

It wasn't the best situation in the world but it wasn't the worst. They only had to survive for two nights and there were enough dry goods to ensure they could. Her spirits lifted.

A comforting warmth filled the small main room. She opened the doors of the two bedrooms so they would also be warm by evening. Maybe they'd be able to finally get a good, restful night's sleep.

She went back to check on Dylan. He continued to sleep peacefully. He needed a haircut and she grinned. She had to fight with herself not to brush his hair away from his ears or allow the tips of her fingers to trail ever-so-softly down his cheeks and neck. He was a handsome man, a fact not wasted on her. But her attraction to him was based on more than appearances, always had been.

There was something special about Dylan. The deep tenor of his voice mesmerized her and she could listen to him speak for hours. The glint in his brown eyes hinted at depths of intelligence and wit she'd only begun to explore. His strength made her feel protected and safe. His kindness wrapped its arms around her heart.

In another time, another place, all of this may have had a different outcome. But...

She shook her head, breaking her trance and bringing her back to reality. She couldn't afford to let down her guard. She felt the pressure of the upcoming trial more potently now than ever. Dylan couldn't protect her even though he'd been doing everything in his power to do so. It was a losing battle. Her father and his crew were more powerful.

Was Frankie Malone working for her father as the marshals believed? She had to admit it was extremely coincidental if he wasn't. But if her father had stooped to using a gang member to silence her, it showed his desperation and cemented her belief that they didn't stand a chance against him.

What a mess they were in! She didn't have a clue how they were going to get out of it.

Her mind flashed on images of a crumpled Selma on the front stoop, of a bleeding, unconscious, probably dead, Bear lying on the ground at their feet. She liked Bear, always had. Pain and loss rushed through her. Now all that stood between life and death was an injured Dylan, who she knew would give his last breath to protect her, and herself, her own wits and skill.

A smile pulled at the corner of her mouth. No, not just the two of them. It was Dylan, herself and God. She realized He had always been by her side these past three years, protecting her, patiently waiting for her to reach out to Him. Well, she was reaching out now. She welcomed the feelings of inner peace after she prayed. No matter what lay ahead, she knew with certainty she was not alone and that made all the difference.

Gently she propped a pillow under Dylan's head.

She should have insisted he go to bed but she knew he wouldn't leave his post at the front door. *Thank you, Lord, for making the human body need sleep or this valiant protector would have never closed his eyes.* Dylan looked comfortable. She had done the best she could do. Hopefully, her efforts had been enough.

Exhaustion cloaked her body. She had a headache to end all headaches and her arm throbbed from all the jarring of her own wounds. She swallowed two pain pills she'd taken out of the first aid kit for herself.

She stretched out on the sofa opposite Dylan's chair. She wanted to be close by should he wake up and need her. She pulled a second blanket she had retrieved from the bedroom over herself and burrowed into the softness of the cushions.

Dawn had come and bright sunshine filtered through the front window. It was going to be a clear, clean, beautiful autumn day.

They were safe.

She stared through the window into the woods.

But for how long?

The sun was setting when Dylan opened his eyes, deep shadows of twilight stretching long fingers across the cabin floor. He couldn't believe he'd slept the entire day. Quickly, he scanned the room in search of Angelina. He found her stoking flames in the fireplace. Although he hadn't moved or made a sound, instinctually she seemed to know he was awake and turned to face him. The fire bathed her in a soft yellow glow. Her beauty snatched his breath away.

"Hi, sleepyhead." A smile touched her lips. "How are you feeling?"

He tried to shove thoughts of Angelina back into the this-is-just-a-witness compartment in his mind but his heart wouldn't let him. Against his better judgment, against all his best efforts, he had fallen hopelessly in love with her.

He glanced away so she wouldn't see the longing in his eyes.

He needed to bury these emotions, remain professional and clearheaded. His sole mission was to get her safely to the trial, not moon over her and think things he had no business thinking. Once she testified she would be free, able to live a normal life again. He owed her that despite what his heart might want.

Again his mind wandered.

His heart wanted him to gather her in his arms, kiss her forehead, and then run. Run fast and far away where no one knew them, where no one could touch them, where they could both start a new life as long as that life was together.

A deep sadness crushed those dreams. He knew she didn't want the same thing. She'd used his feelings for her against him once before, had manipulated him, had humiliated him and had fled. Although fooled once, he wasn't a fool. Angelina moved into the kitchen.

His gaze followed her, noting how she had a dancer's stance and easy gait, making her seem tall and graceful despite her petite frame.

"I bet you're hungry." She gestured to two cans on the counter. "I can offer you dry canned tuna or I can heat up some soup."

Then she lifted a jar and a box. "We have milk, instant coffee and sugar. How blessed can we be?"

He appreciated her attempt to turn their dire circumstances into an adventure but he could see the fear and tension in the depths of her blue eyes. "While you were sleeping, I rigged two pans to some pipe I found in the shed outside." She held it up. "It's not ideal but it'll work well enough to cook something."

He couldn't hide the look of shock and surprise on his face.

"What?" She brought the contraption close for his inspection. "The pioneers didn't have electricity. How do you think they did it?"

He couldn't believe what she'd made out of PVC pipe and masking tape. She was so proud of it. He fought the urge to laugh out loud. As it was, he couldn't hide his grin. He didn't want to hurt her feelings so he chose his words carefully. "I give you an A+ for trying, Angelina. But this could never work. PVC pipe gives off a toxic fume when heated and, worse, if the pipe were to catch fire the flames can't be put out with water. Not a good idea to put it into a fire inside a log cabin."

Her expression looked so crestfallen he felt sorry for her. His little rich Mafia princess had really tried to help. If it hadn't been dangerous, he might have kept his mouth shut and let her try it.

He pushed back the blanket and started to rise. "Give me that."

"Not on your life." She stepped back, determination and defiance shining in her eyes. "I worked all afternoon trying to figure out a workable solution to our problem. It's my invention and that makes it my job to decide what to do with it. So what if it won't work." She shrugged. "Maybe I can find some other use for it." She placed it on the floor beside the door.

"Great idea! A door stop." Dylan laughed in spite of

the throbbing in his head and the shooting pain across his chest when he moved. "I'm going to go outside and start the generator before it gets too dark."

"Generator?" She stared at him, surprise written all over her face.

"All the fishing and hunting cabins are run by generators. Think about it. Did you see any poles, any lines when you were driving these back roads?" He stood. "I'm going to go outside and get ours started before it gets too dark to see. I'll be back in a few minutes."

"Generator?" Her expression darkened. "That's why you were grinning when I showed you my invention. You were laughing at me. Why didn't you say something? You let me go on and on about what a great invention I made when all I did was make a fool out of myself."

"I wasn't laughing at you." He reached out for her hand but she stepped away. "I'm sure you've never been camping in your life, have you?" He could have frozen on the spot for the icy look she sent him. "Yet, you rummaged around and tried your best to find a solution. It doesn't matter if it works or not. You tried. That's one of the things I lo…like about you. You are independent and resilient and strong."

His words didn't ease her anger. He knew she was embarrassed. He didn't know how to make it easier on her.

"I'm sorry." He lowered his outstretched hand. "I think you should be proud of your efforts."

She turned her back on him.

"Angelina…"

She didn't answer or look back.

"I wasn't making fun of you. I thought it was a cute

idea. If it hadn't been PVC pipe, I might have wanted to see if it worked myself."

Silence and showing him her back were her response.

He sighed deeply. "Fine. I'm going outside. I'll be back in a few minutes."

The only sound from the kitchen was the banging of pots.

She tossed the pots on the counter. How could he? He'd played her for a fool. Why didn't he tell her there was a generator? She squeezed a stream of liquid soap into the sink. In a few minutes the generator would be humming and she'd probably be able to get hot water out of the tap. She felt like such an idiot.

Suddenly the lamp beside Dylan's chair and the kitchen light came on.

Great. The generator works.

She fumed a little bit more as she wiped down the counters and then the ridiculousness of the situation seeped through her anger. He must have found it hysterical when she'd shown him two pots, pipe and masking tape. Despite her embarrassment, she could see the humor in the situation and smiled.

It might have worked. If there hadn't been a stupid generator, and then he would have been very happy she'd been smart enough to rig a contraption to feed them even if they would have had to cook outside. At least they would have been able to cook.

Her smile widened.

She was a smart, inventive, enterprising woman and, generator or no generator, she was pretty proud of herself.

Bang!

Angelina gasped and froze. Gunfire! She wished she wasn't so familiar with the sound that she knew instantly what it was.

Another shot.

Dylan.

Someone was shooting at Dylan. Grabbing the PVC pipe by the door, she stepped onto the porch and screamed.

A bear! A big, black, angry bear was running straight at her!

Angelina waved the contraption wildly over her head and in front of her like it was a spear. "Shoo! Shoo! Go away!"

"Get back inside! Close the door!"

Angelina saw the whites of the bear's eyes. That's when she wasn't staring at the animal's teeth. It didn't take any further encouragement to respond to Dylan's command and she ducked back inside. No sooner had she slammed the door behind her, she heard the heavy thundering gait of the large animal as it ran across the cabin porch.

Silence.

Seconds ticked by. She thought she would scream if she didn't hear or see Dylan soon.

When the door opened, she flew into his arms.

He cried out when she threw her arms around him. Realizing that hugging his chest was a bad idea and had probably sent shafts of pain racing through him, she released him instantly and stepped back.

"I'm sorry." Her fingers flew to her lips when she noted the extremely pale tinge to his face and the pool of pain in his eyes. "I wasn't thinking."

He waved her away. "It's okay. I'm fine. Don't worry."

He collapsed in the chair near the door, leaned forward and held his head in his hands.

"Can I get you anything?"

He barely moved but she saw the slight shake of his head.

She ignored his comment and twisted her hands together so tightly her knuckles turned white. "I can't believe a bear was on our front porch. Is it gone? Do you think it will come back?"

"We're in the middle of the woods, Angelina. There's all sorts of wildlife here." Her eyes widened with fear and he hurried to reassure her. "But, no, I don't believe it will be back. I fired into the air and scared it off. It probably was scrounging for a last meal before digging in for winter hibernation."

"That bear was huge! When I stepped outside, I heard you but didn't see you. I didn't know if the bear was running toward you or away. When I closed the door and didn't hear anything, I was afraid you might have been in the bear's path. When you walked through the door I was so relieved I forgot about your injuries. I didn't mean to hurt you."

He waved his hand at her. "It's okay. I'm fine." He took a deep breath, a second one, then sat back in the chair. "What were you thinking? Running outside with a piece of PVC pipe? Just what good did you think that would do?"

"I wasn't thinking. I heard the gunfire. I thought you were in trouble so I grabbed whatever I could find and came to help you."

"Help me?" He sent her an incredulous look. "With PVC pipe and masking tape?" He gestured with his head to the gun cabinet against the wall. "Don't suppose you gave any thought to grabbing something that might really help?"

She glanced at the cabinet, then back at him. "I don't like guns."

He laughed. "Unbelievable! You don't like guns but be careful, bad guys, because my gal can swing a mean pipe." He laughed again almost unable to control himself despite the fact that it was obvious more pain seized him with the movements. "You really are a piece of work, you know that?"

"There you go, laughing at me again." Her mouth twisted in a frown.

"I'm not laughing at you, I'm laughing with you. This will be a story you can hand down to your kids of how Mommy shooed away a bear with pipe and masking tape."

They shared a meaningful look, both lost in their own thoughts at the mention of children. After a heartbeat of awkward silence, Angelina laughed and changed the subject.

"I don't know about you but I'm starved. We haven't eaten since dinner last night. Now that you have the generator running, I guess that means the stove will work."

Dylan nodded.

"Good. So what do you want? Tuna fish and crackers or a bowl of soup?"

"I need to take a few minutes to clean up." He crossed the room to the bathroom. "But if I have a vote, I choose soup and coffee. Dry tuna doesn't do it for me."

"Coming right up."

The grin on her face was infectious and Dylan returned her smile, leaving her to her chore. When he'd finished in the bathroom, he came out to find her sitting in front of the fire. He plopped down next to her. She picked up a bowl of soup and mug of coffee from the floor beside her and offered it to him.

They were finishing their coffee when Dylan said, "Thanks for the soup. I didn't realize how hungry I was."

"How are you feeling?" She spoke softly. "Does your chest hurt?" She stretched out a hand almost automatically and ever so gently touched his bare skin. Her eyes widened. She started to pull her hand back.

He clasped her forearm, stopping her. Their gazes locked. He couldn't fight the surge of tenderness that swept over him. He lowered his head and kissed the inside of her wrist.

"Dylan..." Her tone held a warning but the longing he saw in her eyes told him she wasn't immune to the attraction between them after all.

He raised an eyebrow, waiting for her to tell him to stop.

She didn't.

Dylan drew her closer, cradling her in his embrace. He felt her tremble in his arms like a butterfly in danger of flitting away. He bowed his head and brushed his lips against hers. He felt her catch her breath.

He smiled against the softness and fullness of those lips he'd wanted to kiss for years. He gave her an unhurried kiss.

"Dylan..." She gently pushed away. "We shouldn't. We can't."

Reality hit him like a sledgehammer. She was rejecting him, again, and it stung. But she was right. This shouldn't be happening. His job was to keep her safe and deliver her to the courthouse Monday morning where he would leave her behind and never see her again. He was crossing a line and it had to stop, now.

She moved away, picked up a poker and tended the fire. After a moment, she glanced back over her shoulder, her eyes lighting on his chest and a deeper flash of red tinged her cheeks. She turned her head away and resumed poking at a fire that didn't need any tending.

"I couldn't salvage your shirt. I had to cut it off. But when I was looking for supplies earlier I noticed that Bear has some shirts hanging in his closet. They'll probably swim on you, but at least they'll keep you warm."

Without another word, he went into one of the bedrooms and retrieved a shirt. Gingerly he slipped on the heavy plaid flannel, shards of pain shooting through his chest when he raised his left arm. He cinched the waist, tightening his belt to the last hole, yet the excess material puffed out like an ancient pirate shirt. He rolled the sleeves to his elbows in an attempt to make the gentle giant's clothes look more like a shirt and less like a winter coat. He caught his reflection in the mirror over the dresser.

He remembered the last time he'd seen Bear wear this shirt. It was on their final fishing trip up here. Bear had caught a record-size trout, lost it and spent the night telling the-one-that-got-away story over and over again.

If he wasn't careful, grief would consume him. Bear had been more than a partner, much more. He was a best friend, a father figure. He couldn't believe the man was gone. Didn't dare hope maybe he wasn't, maybe the arriving paramedics had managed to save him. But Bear's closed eyes, the number of wounds, the significant amount of blood loss?

Two partners. Dead. Two partners too many.

He'd promised Bear he'd celebrate with him at his retirement party. A promise he hadn't kept. He'd also promised Angelina that he would protect her and get her to the trial. He'd been unable to keep his first promise but he'd die before he'd break his second one. He grimaced in pain, touched the bandage on his chest and realized that he almost had.

FOURTEEN

"Now that the generator is working and we have lights, I'm assuming there is a hot-water heater someplace and we have hot water, too."

Dylan nodded.

"Good. I'm going to grab one of Bear's shirts, get out of these dirty clothes, and take a shower."

Angelina could feel his eyes on her back as she left the room. Had she heard him correctly earlier? Had he really said "my gal" when he'd been teasing her about the PVC pipe? That sounded like a man who cared about her—a man she had used those feelings against and betrayed.

And what was it with those kisses? For the first time in her life she understood what the term "curled her toes" meant. After all that had passed between them and three years absence, could Dylan still have feelings for her?

She chewed on her lower lip.

And if he did, what did she want to do about it? Did she feel the same way? After everything that had happened, everything still happening, was it even possible they could build a lasting and true relationship?

Her feelings were a jumbled mess right now. She didn't trust herself to know what she wanted. She sighed heavily. She just knew that Dylan mattered, his health, his life. He mattered. She wasn't going to torment herself any more tonight asking herself why.

When she finished her shower she came into the main room, plopped onto the sofa and continued to dry her hair with a towel. Her face scrunched when she glanced across the room at Dylan.

"What are you doing?" She tried to keep tension and fear from her voice.

"I'm making sure we're prepared." Dylan closed the gun cabinet, his arms full of weapons and ammunition. He crossed the room, lowered a rifle to the floor and, with one arm free, held out his hand.

She stared at the small black object in his palm.

"Take it."

She recoiled. "I can't."

"Yes, you can." He thrust it into her hand. "It's easy to handle, easy to hide, is fully loaded and will stop whatever or whoever you are trying to stop."

She stared at the gun, then offered it back. "I have never fired a gun and don't intend to start now."

He ignored her protests, picked up his rifle and sat back in what Angelina humorously thought of as his "sentry" seat.

"I don't expect you to have to use it." Dylan reloaded his handgun and loaded the rifle. "But if the moment comes when your life depends on you squeezing that trigger, then squeeze the trigger. Understand?"

His eyes bore into her. She knew there was no way she could win this argument. He showed her where the safety was, how to use it, and reminded her to release it before she tried to fire. She tucked the weapon into her purse lying on the floor beside the sofa. She nodded but had already made the decision that she would never use the gun—unless Dylan's life depended on her. She prayed that wouldn't happen.

Dylan's laugh drew her attention.

"What?" He was staring at her. She looked down at herself and couldn't find anything particularly funny.

"Bear's clothes may be too big for me but on you they look like you're wrapped in a blanket with buttons."

She glanced down at herself. He was right. She had rinsed her clothes out, hung them to dry on the shower rod after she'd showered and washed her hair and then donned one of the smallest shirts she could find in the closet. Still, on her body the shirt tails touched her feet. She had had to use the suture kit to turn the sleeves inside out and sew the cuffs to her shoulders just so she could move her arms freely.

She chuckled. "Not complaining. Glad these shirts were here. It felt wonderful to be able to shower." She'd removed her gauze bandage and allowed hot water to run over her face, through her hair, down her back, and it had felt wonderful. She finished drying her hair.

Dylan stared at her intently.

"What now?" When he didn't immediately answer, she continued drying her hair.

"You took your bandage off."

She touched her forehead. "I didn't think I needed it anymore."

He smiled but it seemed almost bittersweet. "But now we don't match."

Her breath caught in her throat and she lowered her gaze.

Dylan was the first to speak, one profound word she'd been expecting but had hoped not to hear.

"Why?"

She didn't know whether to play dumb and pretend he was referring to the bandage she had removed or to face the fact that the man had been patiently waiting for a much deserved explanation for what she'd done that night three years ago.

She saw the question in his eyes. She also saw hurt and disillusionment. He'd hurt enough on her account. He deserved to know the truth. Steeling herself for his reaction, she decided the time was right to confess.

"I didn't believe you could protect me."

"No faith in my marshal expertise?" He chuckled, obviously trying to make a joke out of it, but there was a hint of hurt in his tone.

"That wasn't it."

He arched an eyebrow and waited.

"I thought you were on my father's payroll and had been hired to kill me."

His mouth dropped open. The shock on his face chased away any remnants of doubt she may have still harbored that he was working for her father.

"Angelina..."

He stared at her in disbelief. Had he really heard her say that? He loved her. He could never hurt her. Was she kidding? He had almost given his life to protect her.

Of course, he'd never told her he loved her, never spoken those specific words but certainly she should know by now. He'd told her in a million other ways, hadn't he? The way he looked at her, the way he held her in his arms. Could it be possible that she truly didn't know?

Is that why she'd run? Was she afraid of him?

He huffed, not able to speak an intelligible sentence while his mind strained to process this new information. What had he done to make her doubt him either personally or professionally? Did she really believe he was someone whose badge and integrity were available for sale to the highest bidder? He didn't know which belief hurt most.

He studied her face. There was still an egg-size knot on the side of her forehead from the bullet graze. Her blackened left eye wasn't quite as swollen as it had been four days ago but was still discolored. A purplish mottling crept from the edge of her eye down her left cheek.

His stomach clenched. How could she believe he could do something like this to her? A deep, undefinable ache coursed through his entire body. Love him? What a fool he'd been. She didn't love him. On the contrary, she had the lowest opinion of him that anyone could.

He clasped his hands between his knees, his shoulders bowed, his head bent. "Angelina…" He couldn't find anything else to say.

Tension grew between them with each passing second. Finally, he heard her whisper.

"I saw you."

His eyes flashed to hers. "Saw me? Do what?"

She sat wringing her hands, looking away and then back at him, clearing her throat, saying nothing, then clearing her throat again.

He waited, knowing she was nervous, maybe even scared but he didn't care. His stomach seized as if someone had kicked him in the gut. His chest ached. He hurt…and he needed her to say something, anything that would take this hurt away.

"The day you took me to testify before the grand

jury…do you remember everything that happened that day?"

Yeah. He remembered. She had been in the holding room waiting to testify, claimed she was suddenly sick to her stomach and asked to be taken home. Everything he'd tried to say to convince her to testify before going home fell on deaf ears. She insisted she was too sick and would come back another day. She had been pale. Jittery. Weepy. He'd based it on nerves, on being afraid to face her father, but he'd given in. He'd told the district attorney to present his other evidence and that he'd bring her back tomorrow to testify.

Tomorrow never came, though.

Once they got home, she'd recovered quickly. It hadn't taken her long to home in on his vulnerability to her with kisses, hugs, blue eyes that drowned his soul, convincing him she cared. He'd been thinking with his heart and not his head. He volunteered for night duty and let Bear catch some shut-eye. While he was building a fire, she climbed out the bathroom window and disappeared.

Yeah, he remembered that day. How could he forget?

"I saw you pass the bailiff the note."

Baffled, he searched his memory and came up empty.

"What are you talking about? What note?"

A glimmer of something—looked like hope, possibly happiness—shone in her eyes. "You didn't know, did you? You had no idea what that note said."

Frustrated and reaching his limit, his voice came out harsher than he'd intended. "Cut to the chase, Angelina. What are you talking about? I don't have a clue about a note or any idea what it might have said."

Angelina grinned.

Dylan's frustration level soared. What was he saying that was making her so happy? Confusion was quickly becoming anger.

"I glanced into the hallway. I saw you hand the bailiff a small piece of paper. He walked directly into the room where I was waiting and handed me a note." She knew from his expression he was about to explode. "Because I saw the exchange and the bailiff came into the room immediately afterward I believed it came from you."

Dylan clenched his teeth. Trying to rein in his temper, he lowered his voice and forced himself to appear calm. "What did the note say?"

She blanched and twisted her hands tighter. Then she took a deep breath and repeated the words that had lived in her heart and her mind for the past three years. "Do you think I will allow you to testify? I own cops. I own judges. I own the marshals that pretend to protect you. You will never be able to hide from me."

Dylan experienced his second huge shock of the evening. Thoughts and emotions tumbled through his brain. Where should he even start? What a mess!

Wide, blue, tear-filled eyes stared back at him. He could read the expressions on her face like a book. Fear. Relief. Confusion. Hope.

Welcome to my world, Angelina. I'm fighting with my emotions, too.

He got up, perched on the edge of the sofa and clasped her hand. He felt her fingers quiver and knew he'd have to treat her gently or things would worsen.

"I didn't pass on a note, any note, particularly a threatening one." He gave her a moment to think about his words before he continued. "Why didn't you ask me about it? I thought we were close. I thought we were… friends."

"We were."

"But you didn't say anything. You didn't show me the note." He squeezed her hand. Seconds ticked by. "Did you really believe I would harm you?"

"No." Her answer came instantly almost without thought and that made him feel a little better. "Not really." She shrugged her shoulders. "I didn't know what to think."

His gaze locked with hers. "Listen to me. I never would and I never will harm you."

She hung her head as if she was ashamed. "I know." Her words came out in a whisper.

"If that's true, then why didn't you show me the note and ask me about it?"

"Because I saw you! Don't you understand? I wouldn't have believed it if I hadn't seen you pass the bailiff that paper with my own eyes."

Dylan could feel deep grooves etch at the edges of his mouth as he tried to think back to that day. A heavy sigh escaped his lips when the memory clicked.

"The man dropped the note. I picked it up and handed it back to him."

Dylan remembered the man's hand tremors when he'd accepted the paper. The bailiff had been an older man and Dylan had passed the tremors off as age or a disease process like Parkinson's. He'd been so preoccupied with making sure the safeguards he'd requested for Angelina's safety were in place, he'd missed the biggest threat standing right in front of him.

What a fool!

He washed a hand over his face. "I wish you'd said

something to me." He glanced her way. "But I understand why you didn't."

Angelina smiled. "I know it probably doesn't make you feel any better but I had a hard time believing it. I don't think I ever really did even though I witnessed the exchange."

Dylan sighed heavily. "Is that why you ran? You thought I was planning to kill you?" He couldn't believe how wrong she'd been.

"Not exactly, Dylan. I don't think deep down I believed you wished me any harm."

"Then why run?"

"Because I was convinced you couldn't protect me. Even if you didn't write the note or even know its contents, you still allowed the bailiff to get close enough to kill me if he had wanted to."

Dylan's face drained of blood. She was right. He had. How could he blame her for trying to save her own life?

"And you can't protect me now." Gently she placed her hand on his leg. "I have no doubt you'd die trying, Dylan." A bittersweet smile twisted her lips. "You almost proved it." She leaned back against the cushion. "Your ability and Bear's was never in question."

He glanced at her but didn't interrupt.

"It's my father. He has deep pockets and a long reach." She shivered as though a chill had raced up her spine and pulled the blanket over her. "I don't care how good a marshal you are or how many marshals you have standing guard. How can you possibly keep me safe when you don't know who you can trust? When you can't trust the people working with you?"

A leaden weight formed in his gut. She was right. Look what had happened at the safe house. Only a handful of people had been privy to that location. His boss. His secretary. Maybe one or two others in the office who needed to get the safe house set up. Four other federal marshals. That's it. Only a handful of people. Yet, someone gave Frankie Malone that location. Someone inside the department. They had a mole.

"I wanted to get away, this time not to protect myself. This time to protect you and the others." Her eyes teared. "But I was too late."

He gathered her into his arms, ignoring the burst of pain, and cradled her.

She started to pull away but he stopped her.

"Dylan, you're hurt."

"I'm fine." He smiled into her eyes. "I had a very good surgeon."

Again, she started to rise. "It's got to hurt."

"Don't move away. Not yet." He couldn't disguise the huskiness in his voice. "Please."

She froze and stared intently at him. "You've always played superhero for me, haven't you? In grammar school, you stood up for me when the other kids teased me about having a rich dad. In middle school, you made me that beautiful jewelry case out of a cigar box."

"It wasn't beautiful."

She lifted her head and smiled. "But it was! You'd painted the outside a pale blue and glued pictures of daisies on it. You lined the inside with white silk. Remember?"

"I remember you throwing it at me."

She lowered her eyes. "Because you chose that moment to tell me about my father...and I wasn't ready to hear it."

Now it was his turn to look away. "I was hurt because

you turned down my date request. I was a kid. You hurt me. I wanted to hurt you back. I'm sorry."

She touched his cheek with her fingertips and smiled into his eyes. "Don't be sorry. You were always my superhero, and here you are again—protecting me. Thank you."

Gently, she lowered her head closer to the middle of his chest and burrowed deeper into his arms.

It was foolish and unprofessional. She was his witness, an injured and frightened one. He knew she needed to feel safe. She needed to feel protected. She needed to know he was up to the job.

To do that job he needed to keep his head on straight and forget his heart.

But for this moment, he couldn't. The sounds of the crackling fire, the clean, fresh scent of soap in her hair, the firelight dancing across the softness of her skin touched him deeply in his core and he couldn't let her go. Not yet. Maybe not ever. He drew her closer.

A sound caught his attention. He stiffened and started to sit up.

"Dylan?" She raised her head, her blue eyes finishing her unspoken question.

"Shhh." He placed a fingertip against his lips and listened harder.

Instantly, he released her and stood up. He tried to ignore the fear in her wide eyes when he grabbed the rifle. Again, he indicated silence and hurried to the front door. He put his ear against the wood, listened and then ran to the nearest window. Staying to the side, he lifted the edge of the curtain and glanced outside.

"Go into one of the bedrooms. Now."

She sprang to her feet. "What's going on?"

"Hide in the back of one of the closets. Cover yourself with blankets and anything else you can find. Whatever you do, don't come out, no matter what, unless I call you. Understand?"

"Dylan, I…"

"Understand?" His tone brooked no room for discussion.

She grabbed her blanket and ran.

FIFTEEN

Dylan peered out the edge of the window. The car continued to creep forward on the dirt road. No one should be out here. This wasn't fishing season. There weren't any hunting cabins in the area. This car was coming here.

Tension tightened his spine. His index finger twitched against the metal trigger. How had they found them? No one knew about this cabin. No one but Bear. Even if Bear had lived, there was no way he was the mole.

So how did someone find them?

The car pulled up out front and doused its headlights. Whoever it was, they weren't trying to hide their arrival. Probably because they knew if there were enough of them it wouldn't matter. He was their only barrier between them and the witness. They'd probably know he was wounded, too.

Maybe their lack of stealth was a scare tactic to put him on edge. Make him feel at a disadvantage. If it was, it worked.

He glanced over his shoulder. Angelina hadn't taken her purse into the bedroom. The thought bothered him.

She didn't have the gun. She wouldn't be able to protect herself if anything happened to him.

He straightened his spine. He'd have to make sure nothing happened to him.

The car headlights went back on. The driver flashed them on and off, then honked the horn.

Dylan frowned, not sure what was going on. Whoever this was, they weren't acting like one of the bad guys. He didn't open the door. He didn't move from his post at the window. He watched and he waited.

The driver cut the engine. A second later the door opened and the dome light illuminated the person inside.

Selma.

He lowered his weapon but kept it at his side. How did she know to come here?

Bear. Maybe he was alive. Maybe he had given her directions to the cabin.

He studied the car. No one else emerged. There should be at least two marshals. The boss never would have sent just one...and if Bear had sent her, a good marshal would have brought another person. Something didn't feel right.

Slowly he opened the cabin door and pointed the rifle at Selma. "Stop where you are."

She froze.

Slowly she raised her hands in the air. "What's the matter with you? I'm here to help. And I don't appreciate having a rifle pointed at my chest for my trouble."

She didn't move or do anything suspicious. She simply waited.

"How did you find us?" His mind tossed a half dozen scenarios but he didn't like any of them.

"Dylan McKnight, I am not going to stand out here in the dark, in the cold, being interrogated by you. Now put down that rifle. I'll answer your questions inside."

She lowered her hands and took a step forward.

Dylan cocked the rifle, lifted it to shoulder level, ignoring the excruciating pain in his chest, and aimed it right at her.

"I don't believe this." She put her hands on her hips and stared him down. "I am coming in. If you want to shoot a federal marshal, then do it." Without another word, she pushed past him and walked into the house.

He followed on her heels and almost tripped over her when she stopped abruptly.

"You, too?" Selma raised her hands again.

Dylan peered around her. Angelina stood by the sofa, aiming the gun he'd given her straight at Selma.

"Don't shoot, Angelina." Immediately Dylan moved to her side and removed the pistol from her trembling hands. "I thought I told you to hide until I called you."

"I thought you might need my help." She blinked hard. "I didn't realize it was Selma."

Selma lowered her hands. "What's wrong with the two of you? Have you lost your minds?"

Angelina looked sheepish. "Sorry I aimed the gun at you. I was afraid." She was so glad to see the woman alive she wanted to hug her but restrained herself. "We thought you were dead."

"I'm not."

"Obviously," Dylan replied. "But you still haven't answered my question. How did you find us?"

Selma shot him an annoyed look and glared at the rifle. "And you haven't put down your weapon."

An uncomfortable standoff settled between them.

With a heavy sigh, Selma reached over and grabbed Angelina's purse off the sofa. She pulled at the lining, withdrew a button-sized device and held it palm up in her hand.

"Remember this? You put a GPS locating device in her purse in case she took off on you again."

Dylan leaned down and rested his rifle against his chair.

"You bugged my purse?" A look of shock crossed Angelina's face.

"He wouldn't be much of a marshal if he hadn't after your last escapade," Selma answered before Dylan could.

A myriad of emotions flashed across Angelina's face—disappointment, surprise, understanding, anger. Anger won but she turned her wrath on Selma instead of Dylan. "Why aren't you dead? I saw you lying in a heap in the front of the house."

Selma threw her head back and laughed. "Sorry to disappoint you, princess. I fell and hit my head on the front step. It knocked me out for a few minutes. When I woke up, the cavalry had arrived. Fire trucks. Police cars. Ambulances. It was a regular first responder circus. And, lo and behold, the two of you were long gone."

"Bear?" Dylan held his breath. He didn't want to know but couldn't not know.

"Last I checked, Bear made it out of surgery and is going to be fine." She shrugged. "Looks like you lost a partner, anyway, though. He's going to have a prolonged recovery. That gut wound almost did him in. He'll be in rehab for a while and then he'll probably move his retirement date forward. I would if I was him. When you're that close to the gold watch, why take any more chances?"

Dylan collapsed into his chair and breathed a heavy sigh of relief.

Bear is alive. Thank you, God, for answering my prayers.

Selma, feet planted squarely apart and arms crossed, glared at Dylan. "You want to tell me why I received such a warm reception?"

"There's a mole in the agency."

"Duh, you think?" Selma relaxed and sat down. "What was your first clue? The fact that our safe house didn't turn out to be so safe?"

He ignored the snarky tone in her voice. "Who knows you're here? Did you report in to the boss?" Before she could answer, he locked his gaze with hers. "Why did you come alone?"

"Let me see." She put an index finger against her chin as if she needed to think hard about her answer. "Because there's a mole." She stopped throwing sarcastic barbs his way. "Relax. I didn't tell the boss. I didn't tell anyone. And I didn't bring anyone because we are running low on people we can trust."

Dylan relaxed. He had to admit he was happy to see his colleague. He'd need her help when they moved Angelina to the court house on Monday.

"Would you like a cup of coffee?" Angelina moved to the kitchen. "I made a fresh pot right before you arrived."

It didn't take long for Angelina to pour everyone a mug. She even put crackers and dry tuna fish on a plate in front of Selma. "Are you hungry? I know it isn't much but we're a bit limited on dry goods. I can heat up a bowl of soup for you."

Selma laughed and looked at Dylan. "What do you know? Our mafia princess knows her way around a kitchen. Imagine that."

"I wish you would stop calling me that." Angelina sat on the sofa beside her. "I'm not a mafia princess and I resent that tag."

"I call them like I see them." Selma challenged her. "Tell me you aren't. Didn't Daddy send you to expensive boarding schools? Didn't you live in an expensive home? Didn't you have everything laundered money could buy?" Selma sipped her coffee.

"Don't start," Dylan commanded. "Angelina doesn't deserve to be treated like a criminal. She hasn't done anything wrong."

Selma studied Dylan's expression for a moment, then turned to Angelina. "He's right. I have to keep reminding myself that you're on our side. I guess it was the disappearing stunt you pulled three years ago that has left a bad taste in my mouth." She reached for a cracker and scooped tuna on it. "By the way, where were you when the fire started? When Bear came to get me, your bed was empty. When I saw you in the foyer you were fully dressed including jacket, shoes and purse. Were you going somewhere?"

Suddenly Dylan understood. Selma knew Angelina had been trying to sneak out. If it hadn't been for the fire, she might have achieved that goal, which would have finished Dylan's career and put a black mark on Selma's. No wonder she wasn't happy with their witness at the moment.

"I was trying to help." Angelina worried her lower

lip with her teeth. "I wasn't running away for myself. I didn't want any of you hurt on my behalf."

Selma frowned. "Here's a novel idea. If you want to help, try doing what we ask. It would make our job a lot easier."

Angelina nodded. "I will. I promise."

"Good." She took another bite of the tuna cracker. "Just don't expect me to believe you." She changed the subject. She scrunched her face and stared at Dylan. "Nice gauze bandage you have on your forehead. Anything I need to worry about?"

He shook his head. "Only a graze."

"I noticed you're favoring your left arm. Were you injured?"

"I took a bullet in the chest. Angelina cleaned it up for me. Dug out the bullet. I'll be fine."

Selma let out a low whistle and smiled at Angelina. "Wow! There's no end to your talents." She turned her attention to Dylan, concern evident in her expression. "How badly are you hurt? Can you travel? Can you drive? Will you be able to fire a weapon if it's necessary?"

"I didn't have any trouble drawing on you, did I?" He'd never admit to her how difficult raising that rifle had been or the amount of pain he was hiding from her even now.

"Point taken. Still, I'd feel better if it had been in your shoulder rather than your chest. Let me take a look."

Dylan held up his palm. "I'm fine, Selma. Angelina did a good job stitching me up. I'll have no trouble doing my job."

"Angelina stitched you up? Better be careful, princess, you keep being so helpful I might have to rethink my opinion of you."

Angelina ignored her, gathered the empty mugs and carried them into the kitchen. "Do you have any news, Selma? Did they catch the people who started the fire?"

"Some of them," Selma answered. "They caught the one who mattered. A trooper friend of mine assured me that Frankie Malone won't be a threat anymore."

"What?" Dylan peered at her.

"Frankie was pulled over on the Garden State Parkway for speeding. The highway patrol didn't have any idea yet about the fire or his role in it. But Frankie was stupid and shot at the officer. A pursuit ensued. Frankie's car flew off the road. The man's dead."

Angelina gasped.

"Are you sure?" Dylan asked.

"Short of going to the morgue and seeing him myself, I'm sure."

Dylan glanced over at Angelina. The haggard look on her face and stooped shoulders concerned him. He couldn't be sure but it looked as if she was ready to cry.

Cry? Over Frankie Malone's death? No way.

"Angelina? Are you okay?"

"No, I'm not okay. I didn't want Frankie to die."

Angelina saw the confusion on their faces and hurried to explain. "I'll never get my answers now. I'll never know for sure whether he was the one who shot Maria."

"I'd say it's pretty certain that he did. It was his motorcycle that forced us off the Garden State," Dylan said.

"He definitely torched the safe house. That makes him Bad Guy Number One in my book." Selma crossed her legs and leaned back as if that was all she had to know to make him Maria's killer.

"But it doesn't make sense." Angelina threw a dish towel on the counter and rejoined them in the living room. Sitting down next to Selma, she glanced back and forth between them. "If Frankie killed Maria for revenge because she broke up with him, what does that have to do with me? Why would he chase us on the interstate? Why torch the safe house?" She held up her palm to stop them before they could speak. "Don't tell me because he was working for my father."

When she had their attention, she continued. "He might have been on my father's payroll as a drug dealer or numbers runner or whatever. But my father would never have trusted someone so low in the structure of his organization to carry out such an important assignment. And neither one of you believe it, either." She leaned back and released a heavy sigh. "Now that Frankie is dead, we'll never get the answers we need."

"I know exactly why Frankie did what he did."

Selma's voice grated on Angelina's nerves like fingernails on a chalkboard. She wished she could wipe the smug look off the woman's face.

"And, yes, Angelina, you were the target."

Angelina hated this cat-and-mouse game. Selma didn't like her, never had, probably never would. That's okay. Marshals didn't have to like the people they were protecting, they just had to protect them. But Selma took pleasure in taunting her every chance she got and she wished she would stop.

"Spit it out, Selma." Frustration and annoyance rang in Dylan's words. "What do you know and how do you know it?"

"Last night the cops picked up two of the men who helped Frankie torch our safe house. According to a trusted friend of mine," Selma said, "one of the men sang like a canary hoping to make a deal for a lighter sentence with the district attorney."

"And?" Dylan's eyes were riveted to the woman.

"Frankie's plan was to kill Angelina, then go to Baroni and brag that it was his actions that saved him from a death sentence. He believed the capo would show his gratitude by making him a 'made man,' moving him from the bottom rung of the gang he worked in to one of the top rungs in the organization."

"I'd heard Frankie was stupid but if this is true I had no idea how stupid." Dylan shook his head. "Baroni would never reward an underling for a hit he hadn't sanctioned, let alone one on his own daughter. If successful, he would have orchestrated his own death sentence."

Selma nodded. "I agree. But there you have it."

"And Maria?" Angelina twisted her hands together. "Did Frankie date Maria just to get close to me?"

She thought about how happy her friend had been in the beginning of the relationship. The thought that none of it was real, that Frankie had played on Maria's emotions for nothing more than information and proximity to her broke her heart.

"It looks that way," Selma said.

"But why kill her?" Angelina couldn't hide the anguish in her expression.

"Maybe he hadn't intended to kill her." Dylan shot her a sympathetic glance. "Both of you were standing close to each other on that beach, both of you were shot.

It may have been as simple as Maria being in the wrong place at the wrong time."

A shaft of pain traveled through Angelina's body. A random act did nothing to ease the torment she felt that she'd had any role at all in her best friend's death. Sighing heavily, she looked back and forth at both marshals. "At least the worst is over. Bear is recovering. Neither of you were killed. Frankie is dead. Now we can relax until the trial on Monday. We're no longer in danger."

"Are you kidding me?" Selma asked. She sat up straighter and locked her gaze with Angelina's. "Word on the street is that your father is more determined than ever to find you. Money is flowing. Big money. A small army is looking for you. Your father is not going to allow you to testify on Monday. Not if he can help it. You've never been in more danger than you are right now."

SIXTEEN

"Here, thought you might need this." Selma threw a quilted bag on the bed.

Angelina looked inside. Pajamas. A change of clothes. Shampoo. Lipstick. Moisturizer. She tilted her head and stared at Selma. She couldn't figure the woman out. One minute she'd be sarcastic, snippy and downright mean. Then she'd do an about-face and be thoughtful and kind.

"Thanks for these items." She had to admit that sometimes she deserved to be on the receiving end of Selma's sharp tongue. An escape may have saved the woman's life but it would have hurt her career and no one seemed more career-oriented than Selma. She never spoke of having any family. The few friends she did mention were all fellow lawmen. To a person who put their job ahead of everything else, getting a black mark on her career could be a fate worse than death, she supposed.

Selma shrugged. "We fled the house with nothing but the clothes on our backs. I thought by now a little feminine touch might go a long way to making you feel better."

Angelina smiled. "I didn't think you cared how I felt."

Selma bristled. "I don't."

She rolled her eyes.

"If you're happy, and maybe a little bit grateful, I might be able to rely on you to do the right thing." Selma shrugged again. "A gal can hope."

Angelina opened the jar of moisturizer and raised it in a toasting motion. "Thanks, again." She didn't waste any time rubbing the precious cream on her hands and arms.

Selma sat on the edge of the bed and watched. The woman looked as though she wanted to say something.

"What?" Angelina pulled her knees up on the bed and waited.

"Bear frequently teases Dylan. He calls him a superhero."

Angelina nodded. "Yes, I know. I've heard him, too."

Selma stared intently at her. "Bear told me that you're Dylan's kryptonite."

Color rose in her face. Did Bear really think that? Did he really believe that Dylan's proximity to her could be deadly?

Angelina looked away. "That's just silly. Dylan is not a superhero and I am certainly not kryptonite or any other rock or mineral." She smoothed the moisturizer on her legs and tried to act as if Selma's words hadn't hurt.

"Dylan's not up to his job."

Angelina recoiled with shock. "What are you talking about? Dylan's done a wonderful job. He's kept me safe at great risk to himself. How dare you criticize him!"

Selma smiled like a cat who'd enjoyed a dish of

heavy cream. "So it's not one-sided. You have feelings for him, too?"

Angelina frowned and went back to moisturizing her legs. "I don't have to have feelings for anyone to appreciate the job they're doing." She hesitated. "I'm grateful for the work you've done, and Brad and Donna and Bear. Everyone has put their life on the line for me." She looked into Selma's eyes and spoke sincerely. "I'm grateful to all of you. It's a hard job and, I imagine, a thankless one."

Selma leaned back against the headboard and folded her hands in her lap. "I'm not looking for gratitude. I'm just doing my job. But I needed to know if Dylan's feelings were returned. I can see by your immediate defense of him that they are."

"What kind of game is this?" Boy, the woman annoyed her. She was grateful for the protection but she certainly wouldn't miss her when her services were no longer needed. "Besides, what makes you think Dylan has feelings for me? He's been nothing but professional through this entire ordeal."

"Any idiot can see the way he looks at you. He's fallen for you and it's written all over his face."

"You have an active imagination, Selma." She closed the lid on the jar and placed it back on the nightstand.

"Really?" Selma studied her. "You wanted to leave. You had a perfect opportunity to do it."

Angelina glanced her way but didn't comment.

"I'm sure with the injuries that he sustained he must have slept for a while, maybe even lost consciousness a time or two."

"So?" She stared down at her hands.

"You could have run, disappeared again. After being

forced off the road and then having the safe house torched, no one would have blamed you for trying to get as far away from all this craziness as you could—including me." Selma caught her eye. "But you didn't. You stayed. You tended Dylan's injuries. You watched over him. You never left his side."

"He was hurt. What did you want me to do, let him bleed to death? Anyone else would have done the same thing."

Selma smiled. "No. Anyone else would have been scared and run for the hills. You care as much for him as he does for you." She leaned closer and pointed across the room. "That's why you are going to climb out that window and leave with me."

Angelina's mouth dropped open. She couldn't believe what she'd heard. "What are you talking about? I'm not climbing out of any window with anyone and especially not without Dylan."

"If you care about him that is exactly what you will do." The conviction in her voice gave Angelina pause.

"Dylan is doing his best to hide it but the man is in pain, severe pain." Selma stood and paced the room. "He wouldn't let me see his chest wound but it doesn't matter. I can see the way he cradles his left arm close to his body. I see the grimace on his face when he's moved too fast or twisted the wrong way."

"He was shot in the chest. Of course he hurts." Angelina didn't know where this conversation was headed but she didn't believe she was going to like it.

"I wasn't kidding when I told you that your father is spending a substantial amount of money in many different venues for leads to your location."

"Well, he doesn't know this location. Only Bear knows."

"Only Bear?" Selma frowned at her. "That's how I found you. Right?"

Angelina's face blanched. "You followed the transmitter. You have to destroy it. Now!"

"I already have." Selma spoke to her as if she was a youngster incapable of understanding grown-up stuff. "I destroyed it when I went out to the car to bring in this bag."

Angelina breathed a sigh of relief. "Great. So what's the problem? We're safe here."

"Yes, we are. But what about tomorrow?"

She sent Selma a baffled look. "Tomorrow?"

"We have to leave for the city tomorrow morning so we can be ready for court first thing Monday. What do you think is going to happen when we roll into New Jersey? Your father's territory? We won't last a minute before we'll be spotted and someone will turn us in. What do you think will happen to Dylan then?"

"I don't understand."

"He's injured. He's hurting. Don't you think I saw it in his eyes when he held that rifle on me? Why do you think I didn't take it as a viable threat and walked right past him? Because he isn't a threat to me or anyone else in his condition. And he certainly is not a threat to the people your father has looking for you." Selma sat back down on the edge of the bed. "But they are a threat to him." She folded her hands and leaned forward. "Listen to me. He can't handle his weapon properly. He can barely stand the lightest jostling now before he's hit with waves of pain. What do you think is going to happen if he has to run? If he needs to duck down or dive behind something for cover? He won't be able to do it and will be the first one to fall in a gun battle. Do you want that to happen?"

Images of the shoot-out at the house raced through her mind. Running. Crouching behind vehicles. Her stomach turned over.

"He'll die trying to protect you. Bear is right. You are his kryptonite."

The truth in Selma's words stole Angelina's breath away. She couldn't let anything happen to Dylan. "What do you want me to do?"

"Leave with me. Tonight. After he falls asleep."

"He'll hear us before we get ten feet down the drive."

"Not if he's asleep." Selma took a small vial out of her pocket. "This is a mild painkiller, works as a sedative. I'll slip this into a drink and make sure he takes it."

Angelina stared at the brown bottle. "You came prepared with a sedative?" Suspicion shook her bones. "Why would you do that?"

"We had four men burn down our safe house, cover our exits, and open fire on us. Bear was critically injured. If I hadn't fallen and cracked my head on that concrete I probably would have been shot, too. It stood to reason that one of you, if not both, had been hurt in some way during the hail of bullets we endured." She lifted the bottle. "I brought these painkillers from home when I stopped to pack a bag just in case."

She tossed the bottle to Angelina. "Read the label. It's my leftover prescription from about nine months ago when I dislocated my shoulder. They made me tired so I stopped taking them."

A quick glance at the label on the bottle confirmed Selma's words.

"I didn't know what I would find when I got here. I hoped no one was hurt. But if either of you were, then they'd be better than nothing."

Angelina handed her back the bottle.

"Listen to me," Selma insisted. "I know you don't like me. Truthfully, I'm not too crazy about you, either. But I'm good at my job. Some people have families, second jobs, hobbies, other interests. I have my job." Her words demanded Angelina's attention. "My job is to get you to the federal courthouse in Camden in less than twenty-four hours. In one piece. Safe and ready to testify. That is exactly what I intend to do."

Selma sat quietly and waited for her to process everything she'd been told. As much as she hated to admit it, it made sense. Dylan would not back down from any confrontation on any level in his effort to protect her. But at what cost? Selma was certainly not her friend. But she was a diligent federal marshal who prided herself on doing a good job. She wanted to get her to that trial. The least Angelina could do was hear her out.

"What are your plans?"

"Simple. I'm going to slip a couple of these sedatives in Dylan's coffee. Once he falls asleep, we leave."

Angelina felt a headache, a huge one, coming on. "Where will we go?"

"The courthouse."

Angelina shot her a surprised look. "In Camden?"

Selma nodded. "We'll time our arrival at dusk, harder for anyone to spot us, and we'll spend the night in one of the empty offices. I admit it won't be the most comfortable night of our lives but it won't be the first time I've slept on a floor." She chuckled. "It will probably be the first time you've roughed it but you can do it. I have faith in you."

"It's Sunday. The courthouse will be locked."

Selma held up her cell phone. "Did I mention that I have a friend of a friend that can take care of that little problem for us?"

Angelina released a long, low sigh. "What if you're wrong? Dylan never sleeps during the day. If the sedative doesn't work and he's awake, even if we make it to your car and take off, he'll be on our tail in minutes."

"Not if we hide his keys." Selma grinned. "I saw them hanging on a peg by the front door. I'll lift them. He'll never notice they're gone until it's too late."

"We can't leave him here without keys or anyone knowing the location of this cabin."

"We'll leave the keys on your bed. Eventually he'll come in here to look around and he'll find them. By that time, we'll have a good head start and he won't have a clue where we are. Neither will anyone else. We'll be safe for one night."

"Dylan's not going to like this." Angelina worried her bottom lip with her teeth.

"He'll be mad for a minute or two. But he'll meet up with us at the courthouse. Once you testify and this situation has come to an end, he'll get over it."

"I don't know," she said. "I betrayed him once. I don't want him to think I did it again."

"Then leave him a note with the keys. Cover it with *X*'s and *O*'s for all I care. At least, I will have delivered you safely to the courthouse and Dylan will be alive and well."

Angelina stared hard at the woman. She couldn't refute the logic of anything Selma said. "Okay." Reluctant but determined to keep Dylan safe, she nodded. "Let's do it."

SEVENTEEN

Angelina pulled down the visor to block the glare from the setting sun as they crossed the Ben Franklin Bridge. It wouldn't be long now. She tapped her foot against the floor mat and twisted her hands together.

"Relax. We're in the homestretch now." Selma threw her a grin before turning her attention back to the road. "I'm proud of you. You managed to spend the entire day in Dylan's company and didn't give a hint to what we'd planned."

Angelina's stomach clenched. Yeah, she seemed to be good at pulling the wool over Dylan's eyes because he trusted her. He'd soon find out once again she couldn't be trusted. Selma thought he'd get over this newest betrayal. She wished she could be as sure. Would Dylan be able to forgive her for two deceptions? Would he ever be able to trust her again?

They pulled onto the corner of Fourth Street and Market. Selma eased into a parking spot close to the front door.

"What about security cameras? Won't someone see us?" Angelina peered out the window to see if she could spot a camera.

"Try to keep your head down and your face turned away from the camera but don't act weird or do anything to draw attention to yourself. Just get out of the car and walk briskly but normally toward the front door. We're going to look just like any of the other judges or lawyers that show up on a weekend. No one will have a reason to take a second look at the footage."

Angelina did as she was told. Head down. Face turned away. Brisk but normal gait. Up the seven steps, past the white pillars and straight up to the brass-framed glass doors. Piece of cake. Now what?

Selma finished speaking to someone on her cell phone, slid it back into her purse and threw another smile her way.

Angelina wasn't used to this woman smiling—at her or anyone else—and she found it almost disturbing. That thought made her want to laugh out loud.

The door opened. Selma gestured her inside and brought up the rear.

Angelina had only gone a couple of feet when she came to an abrupt stop. "Donna?" Angelina blinked a couple of times. She hadn't expected to see the other marshal.

"Bet you a cup of coffee you didn't expect to see me." Donna grinned.

"Not taking that bet. You'd win. Besides, you know I don't gamble."

"Ahh, Angelina, you don't know what you're missing. Nothing feels better than winning." Donna ushered her through the building.

"There's other ways to win at things than placing bets. I bet it doesn't feel good when you lose some of those bets."

"Truer words never spoken." Donna opened an office door, stood aside and let both women enter.

The three of them sat at the table in the middle of the room.

"Any updates?" Selma asked.

"No. The boss is going crazy trying to find Dylan and his missing witness. He's called every available marshal in on it. I had to plead the flu." She feigned a cough and grinned. "The cops are picking up their snitches to find out if anyone has heard anything on the street about Dylan and, of course, everyone and their uncle is searching for Baroni's missing daughter."

Angelina blanched at the mention of her father's name. She hadn't seen him in over three years and couldn't keep herself from asking, "How is my dad?"

Selma's eyes darted her way. "Don't you go soft and start worrying about Daddy Dearest. He deserves everything and more that is coming his way. If your conscience starts nagging you, I suggest you meditate on the things you and Maria liked to do together."

"Frankie killed Maria." Angelina spat the words, mad at Selma for discounting her feelings for her father.

Selma leaned across the table. "That's right, princess. And why did he? Oh, yes, I remember. He wanted to kill you so Daddy Dearest wouldn't have to go to trial and Maria got in the way."

Donna placed a comforting hand on Angelina's shoulder. "Don't mind, Selma. She gets cranky when the pressure's up."

"Really?" Angelina folded her arms across her chest and glared at Selma. "Could have fooled me. I thought cranky was her normal disposition."

Donna threw her head back and laughed. "She got

you good, Selma. I don't think I've ever seen a witness match you barb for barb before."

Selma frowned at Angelina but turned her attention to more pressing matters. "Thanks again, Donna, for agreeing to help out. You didn't tell the boss, did you?"

"No. I didn't tell anyone. Don't worry." Donna shifted in her seat to make better eye contact with Selma. "How about you? Do you have any idea who fed the safe house location to Frankie Malone?"

Selma shook her head. "One of Frankie's crew confirmed it was an inside job but couldn't give any of the particulars."

"I hope you're wrong. It turns my stomach to think one of our colleagues, possibly our boss, would put us in danger."

"We'll find out soon enough." Selma gestured at Angelina. "Mafia Princess testifies in the morning. Case closed. Then, we investigate our leak."

Donna nodded. "Let's hope it's no one we know."

Selma crossed to the door. "I'm going upstairs. I set up a meet with the US Attorney. He's aware of what's been going on and that we've brought the witness in. He's waiting for me. I'll be back in a bit. Keep an eye on her."

"Will do."

Selma disappeared down the hall.

"I'm glad you're watching me and not Selma. I've had about all of her I can take for a while."

Donna laughed. "She's not too bad. She's married to her job and sometimes that makes her a little…intense."

"Cranky," Angelina said at the same time.

Both women laughed.

"I could use a bathroom break," Angelina said.

"Sure thing. Come with me."

Idle conversation flowed easily between them. Angelina stood at the sink washing her hands when she looked up and caught Donna's reflection standing directly behind her. "I'll be done in just a minute." She held her hands beneath an air dryer. She hated those things. Give her a good old-fashioned paper towel.

"What now?" She turned. The smile slipped from her face. Donna held a gun pointed straight at her stomach.

Dylan's head pounded as if someone literally was hitting him with a baseball bat in a steady, unrelenting rhythm. He kept his eyes closed, held the sides of his head and took a deep breath.

Pain, pain go away. Come again another day.

Even his silly mental singsong couldn't stop the hurt and he groaned aloud.

He breathed in deeply and tried to stay perfectly still.

What was going on? Why did his head hurt like this?

He tried to force his thoughts into focus but they wouldn't obey.

Leaning forward, he bowed his head, clenched his hands together between his knees and waited. Any minute now the fog would lift and he'd actually have a coherent thought.

He tried to open his eyes. At first, they didn't want to listen to him, but gradually he got in one good blink and then another.

Bright daylight poured into the room and momentarily blinded him. All he wanted to do was close his eyes against the light but he didn't. He glanced around.

He was in a cabin. Bear's cabin.

His head spun and his stomach roiled. *What's going*

on? Why am I so foggy? What's happened to me? He felt as if he'd been drugged.

Drugged? That thought made him sit up and pay attention.

The cabin! Angelina!

He threw a glance around the room and saw no one. He started to rise and a wave of pain and nausea made him collapse back into the chair.

Dear Heavenly Father, help me, please.

As each second passed, his thoughts became less jumbled and the events of the day streamed back.

Angelina had fixed him lunch. She'd been quiet and nervous but Dylan hadn't made much out of it. She would be testifying against her father tomorrow. It made perfect sense that she be distracted and probably a bit scared.

Selma.

That's right. She'd shown up last night and was going to help Dylan get Angelina to the courthouse in the morning. Selma had been in the bedroom packing some last-minute things because they'd decided to get a head start and leave after dinner. They had planned to drive to Camden and hole up in a motel nearby.

Dylan had wished they'd had more than the two of them for that task. If he had his way, he'd have an entire task force—FBI, marshals, police—helping tomorrow. But without knowing the identity of the mole, they had no choice but to keep things between themselves.

Where were Selma and Angelina, anyway?

"Selma?"

Dylan stood up. The room spun and he felt lightheaded. He grabbed the arm of the chair to steady himself. When the vertigo passed, he crossed to the bedroom.

"Angelina?"

He paused outside the closed bedroom door, listened, then rapped lightly. "Hello? Are you girls decent? I'm coming in." He opened the door. The room was empty.

He spun around. The place wasn't that big. Where were they? He could see the unoccupied main room and kitchen from where he stood. He quickly crossed to the bathroom and listened. Silence. He opened the door. Empty. He sprang to the second bedroom and flung open the door without pausing to knock. This one empty, too.

What had happened? Where were they? Why was he having such a difficult time remembering? What was the last thing he did remember?

Selma had handed him a cup of coffee and went into the bedroom. Angelina had heated him a bowl of soup. He remembered her hands shook and the soup sloshed over the rim of the bowl when she'd set it down.

"Look what I've done. I'm so sorry." She'd rushed into the kitchen and come back with a dish towel.

He'd stilled her hand as she'd tried to sop up the spilt liquid. "It's okay. It's only soup." He'd smiled but when she looked at him his smile only seemed to make things worse. She became antsy and couldn't seem to make eye contact with him.

"Angelina?" He'd held her wrist until he had her attention. He wasn't sure but he'd thought her blue eyes glistened with unshed tears. "Today is just another day. Nothing to worry about. And tomorrow will be over before you know it. You don't have to be afraid."

"I'm not afraid." She pulled her wrist out of his grasp.

"I'll be by your side every step of the way. No one is going to hurt you." He kept his voice steady, calm, offering her assurances he didn't feel himself.

She nodded and glanced away.

"Dylan, leave the girl alone." Selma stood in the bedroom doorway. "If she's a little nervous, I'd say that's normal given the circumstances but she'll be fine." Selma gestured to his mug. "Finish your coffee. Angelina, come help me in the bedroom."

Angelina had scampered in Selma's direction. Dylan had finished his coffee, ate a little of the soup and then...

He had been drugged!

The realization hit him in the solar plexus. That was why he felt so groggy, why he couldn't remember, why he was so unfocused.

Had Selma drugged him? Or worse, had Angelina?

Dylan moved to the front door as quickly as the pain in his head and chest allowed. Selma's car was missing. The women were gone.

Who was the bad guy here? Had Angelina drugged him, got the drop on Selma and somehow forced her to drive her out of here?

Or was Selma the mole?

And if Selma was the mole, what was she going to do with Angelina?

He reached for his keys and saw the empty peg.

His stomach clenched. A deep, intense pain shot through his heart, a pain that had nothing to do with his physical injuries. He'd promised to keep Angelina safe. He wouldn't be able to live with himself if anything happened to her.

He glanced at his watch. He hadn't been unconscious long. They had maybe an hour head start on him.

Keys. Keys. Where are the keys?

Frantically he moved throughout the cabin tossing cushions, looking under furniture. He found them wrapped in a note lying on Angelina's bed.

His fingers trembled when he opened the letter.

XOXOXO.

His breath caught in his throat. Without another moment's hesitation, he turned and raced to his car.

EIGHTEEN

"Donna? Why are you pointing your gun at me?" Angelina raised her hands. The sink pressed hard against her back. Her eyes darted back and forth. She was trapped with nowhere to go.

"Don't make another sound. Understand?"

Angelina nodded.

"Do what you're told and you won't get hurt." Without lowering her weapon, Donna backed up to the bathroom door, cracked it slightly and checked outside. "Okay, here's the plan. Lower your hands."

Angelina complied.

"Quietly and calmly, the two of us are going to walk right out the front door."

"I don't understand. What's going on?"

Donna ignored her question. Instead she pressed her gun into Angelina's side, hard. "Shut up. If you want to stay alive, do exactly what I say. Now move. Don't try to run. Don't do anything to draw attention to yourself." She shoved her into the hall.

"Why are you doing this?" Angelina asked as they moved toward the exit.

"What did I say? Didn't I tell you to be quiet?" Donna's breath fanned her ear and the poke with the gun became painful. "I don't want to kill you. Believe me, I don't. But I will if I have to."

The blood drained from Angelina's face leaving her light-headed. Her legs quivered, threatening to dump her in a heap on the floor. She couldn't believe this was happening. What was Donna doing? She threw a glance over her shoulder. Where was Selma? She'd sure be glad to see Miss Cranky right about now.

"Move." Another shove, another painful dig into her side.

Within seconds, they were outside. The sun had set long ago and only the outside lights illuminated the darkness.

"Head down. My car's to the left. Move it."

Angelina grabbed the railing to keep from stumbling down the steps as Donna pushed her in the direction she wanted her to go. If she buried that gun any deeper in her side, she was afraid it would accidentally go off.

They reached the car without incident, passing no one going in or out. But it was Sunday evening. Did she really think she'd be able to flag down help? Angelina dared one more glance over her shoulder. Where was Selma when she needed her? Donna fastened Angelina's right wrist to the door handle with a zip tie.

So much for any thoughts of taking her chances and jumping out.

It wasn't until they hit the Atlantic City Expressway that Angelina dared to speak again.

"Please, Donna. Tell me what's going on. Where are we going?"

Donna threw a hurried glance in her direction, then

looked back at the road. "You'll find out soon enough. Just be quiet."

"Are you taking me to another safe house? Does Selma know what you're doing? Does Dylan?"

Donna laughed mirthlessly. "Another safe house? I guess you could call it that. Once I get you to where we're going both of us are going to be safe."

A sense of foreboding seeped through Angelina. She knew without asking. Donna was the mole. Donna was on her father's payroll. Donna was going to kill her and there was not a thing she could do about it.

They traveled several more miles before Angelina dared to speak again. She kept it short and to the point but she really wanted to know.

"Why?"

Donna glanced her way, fear and maybe even a little guilt evident in her expression. "Why does anybody do anything in this world? Money."

That surprised her. She'd spent several days in Donna's company. She'd seemed like a dedicated federal marshal and, truthfully, a fun, pleasant individual she could see herself liking in a totally different social situation. There had to be more to the story.

They'd left the expressway and were driving through less-than-safe neighborhoods. Where was Donna taking her? She didn't have to wait long to find out. The lights from the casinos and the boardwalk loomed straight ahead.

Donna pulled over on one of the side streets, came around the car and opened the door, Slicing off the zip tie. "Don't try anything." Donna took a step back and gestured with her gun. "Get out."

"Where are we going?" Angelina stepped out of the vehicle.

"Up on the boardwalk. Go."

Angelina's hurried glance up and down the street was fruitless. The street was deserted. Her only hope was the boardwalk. People would be coming in and out of the casinos. Even at this hour people would be strolling by, maybe even a patrol officer. And it would be better lit than this back street. Yeah, her only hope was the boardwalk. She didn't need any further encouragement to get there as quickly as she could.

The fresh scent of salt water hit her nostrils almost as soon as her feet hit the wooden walk. The sounds of people talking, laughing, even the tinkling rolls of slot machines hit the air as doors to nearby casinos opened and closed. The ocean breeze lifted several wisps of her hair.

Angelina had always loved the Atlantic City boardwalk and beach. She supposed if she had to choose a place to die it was as good as any. She just wished she could find a way to make that happen decades from now instead of minutes.

Donna grabbed her arm at the elbow and pulled her up short.

Angelina looked her right in the eyes. "What now?"

Donna pointed. "Down the steps and to the left."

Angelina took a second to orient herself and her stomach clenched. Tears burned the back of her eyes. She knew where she was. She'd been in this exact spot less than a week ago. Straight ahead at water's edge she'd lowered Maria's body to the sand, dead from a shot fired from beneath the pier on their left. How ironic that her final resting place would be in the same place.

Sand filled her shoes and weighted her feet as they made their way across the beach into the darkness beneath the pier. When they reached their destination, Angelina pulled her arm away and turned to face her executioner.

"Okay. I'm here. You get to kill me without any witnesses. But at least you can answer a couple questions for me before you do. You owe me that."

Donna's chuckle held no humor. "I don't owe you anything. But it never hurts to ask."

Angelina's eyes couldn't pull themselves away from the barrel of the gun pointed at her.

"You're the mole, aren't you? You're on my father's payroll."

"See. I told Selma you were smarter than she gave you credit for."

"How much money is he paying you?"

"What is it to you?"

Angelina shrugged. "I'm curious. How much is his daughter's death worth? And how high a price tag did he have to pay to twist you from an honorable federal marshal to a low-life criminal like him?"

Donna winced at that latter statement. Apparently her marshal status had been more difficult for her to forfeit than Angelina had suspected.

"Remember that question you asked me earlier?"

Angelina arched a brow in question.

"When we talked about betting… I told you it felt wonderful to win. I didn't tell you how horrible it feels to lose. I got in over my head in gambling debts. I made the mistake of trying to raise the money to pay those debts by hitting the blackjack tables. I lost."

Donna's gaze darted away for a moment and she

could have sworn she saw regret and shame flash across the marshal's face.

"What happened next was straight out of an old movie." Donna harrumphed. "Your father made me an offer I couldn't refuse. All gambling debts forgiven. Clean slate." Donna shrugged. "Like I said, I couldn't walk away."

Angelina glanced to her left. Her eyes searching the stretch of beach for the spot Maria had been shot but she couldn't see it in the darkness. She listened to the crashing of the waves. Felt the spray of cold water against her body as waves hit the pilings under the pier. She offered up a silent prayer.

I'm not afraid, Lord. I know You are with me. I pray if this is Your will that You carry me home in Your blessed arms and please, Lord, don't let Dylan carry any guilt for any of this. Please.

She turned her attention back to Donna. "Why did you bring me here? Poetic justice? Were you the one who shot Maria a week ago from this very spot?"

"All of a sudden you're a chatty one, aren't you? Think I'm going to stand here all night talking and answering endless questions? I'm not."

Tears flowed down Angelina's face. "Did you kill Maria? Why? If I was the target why didn't you just shoot me? You're killing me now. Why did you waste Maria's life?"

"No, I didn't kill Maria. Frankie Malone did that all on his own. Your father didn't sanction that hit." She took a step closer. "Enough talking. Shut up and start walking." She gestured with her gun. "Over there."

Angelina, more confused than ever, took a few steps in the direction Donna indicated, then came up short when she saw a shadow step out from behind one of the pilings. She stared hard into the darkness and the tears streamed harder down her face.

"Dad?" Her voice, a mere whisper, escaped on the ocean air. She wasn't even sure he'd heard her.

"Angelina." Her father stepped closer. He held a weapon in his right hand, his arm at his side, the weapon pointed at the sand.

She locked her gaze with his and straightened her shoulders. "If you're going to kill me, do it. Get it over with."

He came within three yards of her and the moonlight illuminated his features. "Kill you?" He lifted both hands out to the side in a pleading motion. "How could you believe I would kill you? You are my daughter, my flesh and blood. I could never hurt you."

She hadn't expected that answer. Confusion raced through her mind, along with guilt, anger, longing and finally determination. Why couldn't he have been a normal father, a decent guy? She wanted to run to him, wrap her arms around his waist, listen to the timbre of his voice in her ear like she'd heard a million times before when he'd comforted her on a stormy night or held her when teaching her to dance for her school prom. Her heart ached. She loved her father. She always would. But she hated what he'd done, who he'd become. She offered a quick prayer for her father's soul and reminded herself that God, not her, would be his judge.

"It seems to me you went to a lot of trouble and expense to bring me here if you aren't intending to kill me. So why am I here?"

"I can't let you testify tomorrow. You know that."

She saw the hardened glint in his eyes, heard the steel in his voice, and a slither of fear crept up her spine.

"You killed our neighbor, Mr. Cartwright. I saw you."

"Yes, I did. Killing him brought me great pleasure and I would do it again, gladly."

Angelina shook her head. "Why, Dad? Mr. Cartwright was a nice man, minded his own business, kept to himself. He was nice to me, too. Always stopped to talk to me if he saw me in the yard. He'd smuggle me pieces of candy through the fence. What could he have done to deserve to die?"

"He had an affair with your mother and was solely responsible for her death."

Angelina gasped. "That's not true. That can't be true. You told me my mother died of pneumonia when I was two."

"Your mother died because I killed her. No one cheats on me."

"No! That can't be true!" Horror raced through her veins.

"It took me years to prove that Cartwright was the man your mother got involved with but I finally got the proof. When I did, I took great delight in killing him. I only wish I could have killed him more than once."

"What kind of monster are you?"

"Grow up, Angelina. How do you think I reached the heights I did? Because I do not let anyone betray me." Her father sighed. "My only regret was that you saw it. You'd left for the evening. Why did you come back?"

"I'd forgotten something in my room. I grabbed it and started to leave when I remembered that I... I..."

"What?" Her father cocked his head to the side and looked at her.

"I remembered I hadn't kissed you goodbye, so I searched the house looking for you…" Her voice trailed off. Painful memories seized her thoughts. She'd been searching for him for a kiss.

"Oh, Dad." Her voice held all the pain of her heart being torn apart. She met his gaze. "You better kill me, too, because I am going to testify tomorrow."

"You ungrateful little snot. I never heard you complain about the lifestyle you led. Only now are you growing a conscience about the way I earned my money to do it."

"You kill people, Dad. Living, breathing, decent people! Mr. Cartwright isn't the only person who has died because of you. Maria is dead. Dylan and Bear almost died. And all the others, Dad, in your so-called business of extortion, money laundering, drugs. How many others have died at your hand or at your command? I can't believe you even killed my mother!" A sob clenched her throat.

"I won't let you testify." He tried to reason with her. "You will be killing me. *Me!* Is that what you want, Angelina? To kill your own father? If you testify they will find me guilty. You might as well stick that needle in my arm yourself!"

Despair like she'd never known washed over every inch of her. Sobs came with such force they stole her breath. Still, she stood her ground. "I can't let you get away with what you've done. I have to stop you from the things you would still do."

The anger in his voice was colder than ice and stronger than steel. "Oh, I'm not going to kill you Angelina.

But I'm afraid that there may be days ahead when you'll wish I had."

She shot him a questioning look.

"I'm going to send you out of the country. You will be under my protection for the rest of your life. You will have no friends. No family. No husband. No children. No future. But you will be alive…and so will I."

Angelina shook her head and stared at him in disbelief.

"You can't do that." Astonishment and hurt laced her words.

"Watch me."

"Well, excuse me for interrupting this warm family reunion but if it's all right with both of you, I'm leaving." Donna's voice caught their attention. "If I want to salvage my career, I have to get busy and spin a tale of how Ms. Baroni took me by surprise, grabbed my weapon and forced me to drive her to Atlantic City where she made her escape." Donna looked directly at Vincenzo Baroni. "I did what you requested. My business with you is over. My debts forgiven. My slate clean. Right?"

Vincenzo Baroni inclined his head. "That was our deal."

"Good." She stared at him another instant and then turned and walked away.

Vincenzo raised his weapon and aimed at the marshal's back.

"No!" Angelina screamed. She lunged forward and pushed her father's arm away. The gun fired but missed its intended target.

At that same instant, when Donna heard Angelina

yell she spun on her heel, raised her weapon and fired multiple times.

Her bullets didn't miss.

Vincenzo Baroni's body recoiled with each hit. A surprised expression appeared on his face.

"Dad!" Angelina had an overwhelming sense of déjà vu as the blood saturated her father's chest and, almost in slow motion, he crumpled to the ground. She fell to her knees beside him, sand grinding into her skin. She placed two fingers against the carotid artery in his neck to search for a pulse. There was none.

"Dad!" She yanked on his shirt, pulling at him, shaking him, venting her hurt and shock. "Why did you do this? Why?" She kept yelling even though she knew he'd already died and she would never get that answer.

She turned her attention to the marshal. "You killed him."

"He gave me no choice. It was him or me." Donna raised her arm and pointed her gun at Angelina. "Sorry, Angelina, but that's why I have to kill you, too. Nothing personal. You're a witness. If you can testify against your own father, you will have no trouble testifying against me. I can't afford to leave any witnesses, especially you."

"Donna?" Dylan ran forward, his shoes sinking in the sand. "I got here as quickly as I could." His eyes flew immediately to Angelina hovering over her father's body. "What's going on?" He took another step toward Angelina.

"Is that Vincenzo? Is he dead?" He had almost closed the distance between them when Donna called out.

"Stop right there! Don't take another step."

Dylan did as she commanded.

"Now take out your gun and throw it nice and easy over to me."

Dylan hesitated.

Donna smiled. "Do it, Dylan, or I'll put my next bullet into your girlfriend."

Dylan removed his weapon and tossed it onto the sand within Donna's reach.

She bent to the side to pick it up, never taking her aim from Dylan. "Now raise your hands."

He did as he was told. "What's going on? Where's Selma? How did you get involved in this?"

Donna's laugh was harsh and cold. "You two make a great pair. You both ask so many questions it's a wonder you ever get a word in edgewise with each other."

Donna held her gun on Dylan but nodded in Angelina's direction. "Get up and move over there with Dylan."

Angelina stood. "What are you going to do?"

"Stop with the questions and move!"

Angelina slowly moved toward Dylan.

"Run, Angelina!" Dylan lunged forward, pushing Donna's arm up. They fell to the ground, both struggling for control of the gun.

The sound of the gun firing echoed beneath the pier.

Angelina held her breath, her eyes glued to the two immobile figures on the sand.

"Dylan?"

The seconds ticked past. Angelina thought her heart would stop.

Move, Dylan. Dear Lord, please let him be all right and tell him to move.

It took another excruciating second before Dylan moaned and then rolled onto his back.

"Dylan!"

Angelina raced to his side and helped him to his feet. "Are you all right?"

He threw an arm across her shoulders and stared down at the dead body of his former colleague. "I didn't want to kill her. The gun went off during the struggle."

"I was so scared. She killed my father. She would have killed both of us without hesitation if you'd given her the chance."

"Shhh, it's okay." She felt his hand stroke her hair, then slide down her back and encircle her waist, pulling her close. "It's over. You're safe."

Her entire body shook like a leaf in the wind. She clung to him, burrowing her face in his chest, grasping his shirt in a death grip. She looked up and her eyes found his. The expressions on his face moved her deeply. Fear. Relief.

"I almost didn't make it here in time." The huskiness in his voice revealed his inner anguish. "One second longer and…and…" Even in the dimness of the evening she could see his dark brown eyes glistening with unshed tears. She could feel the desperation in his touch as he clasped her against him, holding her tightly in his arms. "One second longer…"

"Dylan, stop." She reached up and cupped the side of his face with her hand. She smiled into his eyes. "You saved me. You kept your promise. You kept me safe. Do you hear me?" She placed her lips against his in the gentlest of kisses and when she had his full attention she smiled again. "You saved me, Dylan McKnight."

He claimed her lips with his own. Passion warred with gentleness, desperation warred with relief, and it seemed he was allowing his kiss to do all his talking for him.

Gently she pulled her head back enough to look him full in the face.

"How did you find me?"

"A tracking device."

"But Selma told me she destroyed the bug you put in my purse."

He chuckled. "She did." He kissed her again, then grinned. "You taste like salt from ocean spray and tears." He dragged a thumb across her cheek, washing away her tears. "But there's no reason to cry. It's all over now. I found you. Selma didn't know about the bug I hid in your shoe."

"You bugged my shoes?"

Both of them looked at her feet.

Dylan laughed loudly. "Yes, I did. After your escape act three years ago, I wasn't taking any chances." He tilted her chin and looked deeply into her eyes.

"Are you mad at me?"

Angelina laughed in return. "Furious." She laced her fingers in his hair, pulled his head down and kissed him back with passion, yearning and hope.

The sound of sirens could be heard in the distance.

Angelina looked at him with a question in her eyes.

"I know you think I'm a superhero, but I called for backup just in case."

"Have you spoken to Selma?"

"I haven't spoken to anyone yet. I was doing my best to follow your tracking device and get here before anything happened to you. I barely took the time to call for help. Thank the good Lord, He got me here in time."

He brushed the hair from her face. "Where is Selma? What happened?"

"Donna told me Selma had the US Attorney's Office investigate the marshal's office. They ran a background check on everyone from your boss to every clerk and marshal that had been involved in the case. Donna knew that when they discovered her debt load and gambling addiction, it would give her motive and expose her. She took me to my father in a desperate attempt to get me out of the picture and wipe her debt clean."

The sound of multiple loud, wailing sirens from the boardwalk area blasted the airwaves.

Dylan kissed her again. "Sounds like help has arrived."

"Let them wait," Angelina whispered, her lips moving against his as she returned his kiss. "We don't need any help at the moment."

Dylan chuckled. "I love you, you know." His expression sobered and his eyes darkened. "I think I always have."

"You think?" Angelina teased him. She buried her nose in his neck and inhaled the male muskiness of his scent. "How will I know when you are sure?"

"Every day of my life I am going to hold you in my arms." Dylan pulled her so close she could feel the pounding of his heart. "And kiss you…" Which he did. "Over…" He kissed her. "And over again." He smiled down at her. "Then when we hit the ripe old age of one hundred, maybe then I'll be absolutely sure not only that you are my soul mate, the woman God intended me to share my life, but the woman I've loved since sixth grade." He tapped his index finger on the tip of her nose. "Only then, after a lifetime of love, will we both know for sure."

Angelina's heart swelled with joy. Finding their way to each other had come with heartache, pain and seemingly insurmountable obstacles, but with patience, determination and a strong faith they'd found their way to the promise of a future filled with hope and happiness.

"Sounds like you've got your work cut out for you," she whispered against his lips. "If I were you, I wouldn't waste another minute."

He didn't need any further encouragement, crushing her against the length of his body, lacing his fingers in her short auburn hair. "Red hair looks cute on you, but I like your dark hair better. It will be good to have the real Angelina home again."

The intensity in his dark brown eyes melted her to the spot.

The sound of sirens from the boardwalk swirled in the air around them. Cold ocean water hit the wooden pier supports and the frigid water sprayed their faces and splashed against their clothes. But none of it mattered. They were lost in their own little world.

Without another word, Dylan lowered his head and claimed her lips.

Angelina lost herself in his kiss. Thinking of nothing and no one, only Dylan and this moment, this kiss—a perfect kiss—the forever kind.

EPILOGUE

October
One year later

"I can't believe you call this fun." Angelina blew a wisp of black hair out of her eyes and adjusted her fisherman's cap. "We've been sitting here for hours. The sun's beating down on us. We haven't caught a thing. And you won't let us talk because you said we'll scare the fish away. How is this fun?"

Dylan laughed. "It is fun. It's relaxing."

Angelina rolled her eyes. "Yeah, about as much fun as standing on a street corner watching traffic."

"Somebody sounds hungry and tired." Dylan took the rod from her hand. "Let me put these away and we'll head up to the cabin and get some lunch."

"Now you're talking." Angelina sprang up. She scrunched her face as if she was disgusted and wiped her hands on her jeans. "Yuck, how can my hands smell like fish when we didn't catch anything?"

Dylan laughed again, secured the fishing poles to the bottom of their boat and helped her step up to the pier.

"I do believe, my little Miss Complainer, that learning how to fish was your idea, not mine."

"I'm not little *Miss* anything. I am Mrs. Dylan Mc-Knight, I'll have you know."

Dylan wrapped his arms around her waist and pulled her close. "I heard a rumor to that effect. Think there's any truth to it?"

Playfully she pushed against him but he didn't let her go. His eyes darkened and his expression sobered.

"Are you happy?"

She wrapped her arms around her husband's waist and smiled into his eyes.

"Ecstatically happy. The past forty-eight hours have been wonderful."

He took her hand and they began the short trek to the cabin.

Sun dappled through the overhead foliage dotting the ground ahead like thousands of diamonds. The brilliant fall colors entranced her with their beauty—golds, reds, oranges, greens. Water lapped gently on the shore and she could hear the occasional sound of a duck. Dead leaves crunched beneath their boots. Angelina took in everything, not wanting to miss a thing, storing it in her memory banks to last a lifetime.

"Are you sorry?"

She shot him a look of surprise. "Sorry? For what?"

"For choosing Bear's fishing cabin for our honeymoon?" He squeezed her hand. "It is your fault you know. I offered you a honeymoon in Hawaii or the Bahamas or anyplace else you wanted to go. Why did you let Bear talk you into coming here?"

She leaned her head against his shoulder for the briefest moment before continuing on their walk. "Because it meant so much to him. He was like a proud papa gifting us with the honeymoon location, strutting around the reception like a peacock."

He grinned at her. "I did say that I offered Hawaii, the Bahamas…"

Angelina laughed. "I'm glad we chose the cabin."

"Yeah, right. Let's spend our honeymoon coming back to a place where we hid out from bad guys. Great memories, Angelina."

She stopped walking and gave him a serious look. "This cabin does hold great memories, Dylan. This is the place where we reconnected. We had the opportunity to talk about the past, get rid of misconceptions, start fresh. This was a place of rest, of healing, of peace. Good memories happened here and I wouldn't want to be anywhere else right now. Would you?"

He smiled into her eyes. "Since you put it that way…"

Angelina wrapped her arm around his waist as they continued their walk. "Besides, I wanted to make Bear happy. I can't forget that we almost lost him. He had a long, painful recovery."

"Yes, he did. But he's a tough old bird."

"It was so much fun seeing him at his retirement party."

He chuckled. "That it was. He was king for a day and basked in every second of it."

"And now the two of you are opening your own security business next month. What a difference a year can make."

They walked the rest of the way in comfortable silence, each lost in their own thoughts. Angelina was the first to break the silence.

"Do you think you're going to miss being a federal marshal?"

"Protecting witnesses that either don't deserve it or don't want to be protected? Dodging bullets? Sometimes having those bullets hit their target?" He scrunched up his face as though considering a major puzzle and then grinned. "Not on your life."

They climbed the few steps to the porch and Angelina reached for the doorknob.

"Hold up, there. What do you think you're doing?" Dylan swept her up in his arms. "A new husband is supposed to carry his wife across the threshold."

Angelina laughed and wrapped her arms around his neck. "You carried me over the threshold yesterday. You're not supposed to do it every day."

He nuzzled her neck and held her tightly in his arms. "Why not? I think we should start a new tradition. I think the groom needs to take every opportunity he can find to hold his lovely…" he kissed her "…beautiful…" he kissed her again "…wonderful wife in his arms."

She clung to his neck with one arm and cupped his face with her free hand. "I love you, Dylan McKnight."

"You better." He grinned back at her.

She reached down, turned the knob and gave the door a shove.

Once inside, Dylan settled her on the sofa. "Wait right here."

"Where are you going?" she called as he moved toward the bedroom.

He paused in the doorway. "Patience, love. Good things come to those who wait."

True to his word, he was back in a few minutes. He knelt beside her.

"What are you up to?" she asked, noting that he was hiding something behind his back.

"I have a present for you."

She clapped her hands together and giggled. "You know how I love presents. Let me see."

He placed a gaily wrapped gift in her lap.

"Can I open it?"

He nodded.

She pulled at the ribbon and then paused. "I feel bad. I don't have a gift for you."

He laughed and waved his hand. "Just open it."

She peeled back the wrapping paper and then gasped. Nestled in a bed of tissue paper rested a cigar box painted pale blue with pictures of daisies glued all around.

"You kept it! After all these years, I can't believe you still have it."

He sat back on his heels. "I could tell you that I threw it in the top of my closet and forgot about it until recently."

"You could." But her tone told him she didn't believe him.

He reached out and captured a strand of her hair in his hand. "Or I could be truthful and tell you that I've loved you all of my life. Our lives may have veered apart a couple of times, but we've always seemed to find our way back together."

Gently she lifted the lid and drew another surprised breath. Lying on the white silk was a locket shaped like a heart. "What's this?" She picked up the piece of jewelry, the delicate chain slipping through her fingers.

"Open it."

Angelina hit the clasp and found four small chambers

inside, two of them occupied with their pictures and two empty. Tears filled her eyes and she smiled at him.

"And the empty spots?"

"For our children. We'll put their pictures inside and you will always have our family right next to your heart."

"Two children, huh?" Her smile brightened. "And what if I want a larger family?"

He grinned. "I hoped you might say that." He reached out and showed her a tiny loop at the bottom of the locket. "I made sure we could add additional lockets."

Angelina wrapped both hands around his neck and pulled him close. She kissed him, hoping this kiss would tell him everything he needed to know, would let him feel all the joy and love she harbored for him in her heart.

"I love you Dylan McKnight."

"I love you Angelina McKnight." He whispered against her lips. "And I always will."

* * * * *

Dear Reader,

When writing this book, I wanted to explore some of the issues surrounding trust, judgment and justice. Angelina had to testify against her father after witnessing a murder. But she also struggled with her feelings about that part of the man that wasn't an organized crime lord but simply a dad.

Sometimes the people that hurt us most can be found inside our own families. Although they're not trying to kill us like the characters in this story, they may have hurt us deeply just the same. I believe no one is all bad. It is the good part of that family member that is loved.

Thank you for reading this story. I hope it left you with thoughts to ponder while taking you on an enjoyable romantic adventure.

I can be reached at diane@dianeburkeauthor.com.

Diane Burke

REQUEST YOUR FREE BOOKS!

2 FREE RIVETING INSPIRATIONAL NOVELS
PLUS 2 FREE MYSTERY GIFTS

Love Inspired®
SUSPENSE
RIVETING INSPIRATIONAL ROMANCE

YES! Please send me 2 FREE Love Inspired® Suspense novels and my 2 FREE mystery gifts (gifts are worth about $10). After receiving them, if I don't wish to receive any more books, I can return the shipping statement marked "cancel." If I don't cancel, I will receive 4 brand-new novels every month and be billed just $4.99 per book in the U.S. or $5.49 per book in Canada. That's a savings of at least 17% off the cover price. It's quite a bargain! Shipping and handling is just 50¢ per book in the U.S. and 75¢ per book in Canada.* I understand that accepting the 2 free books and gifts places me under no obligation to buy anything. I can always return a shipment and cancel at any time. Even if I never buy another book, the two free books and gifts are mine to keep forever.

123/323 IDN GH5Z

Name _____ (PLEASE PRINT)

Address _____ Apt. #

City _____ State/Prov. _____ Zip/Postal Code

Signature (if under 18, a parent or guardian must sign)

Mail to the **Reader Service:**
IN U.S.A.: P.O. Box 1867, Buffalo, NY 14240-1867
IN CANADA: P.O. Box 609, Fort Erie, Ontario L2A 5X3

**Are you a current subscriber to Love Inspired® Suspense books
and want to receive the larger-print edition?
Call 1-800-873-8635 or visit www.ReaderService.com.**

* Terms and prices subject to change without notice. Prices do not include applicable taxes. Sales tax applicable in N.Y. Canadian residents will be charged applicable taxes. Offer not valid in Quebec. This offer is limited to one order per household. Not valid for current subscribers to Love Inspired Suspense books. All orders subject to credit approval. Credit or debit balances in a customer's account(s) may be offset by any other outstanding balance owed by or to the customer. Please allow 4 to 6 weeks for delivery. Offer available while quantities last.

Your Privacy—The Reader Service is committed to protecting your privacy. Our Privacy Policy is available online at www.ReaderService.com or upon request from the Reader Service.
We make a portion of our mailing list available to reputable third parties that offer products we believe may interest you. If you prefer that we not exchange your name with third parties, or if you wish to clarify or modify your communication preferences, please visit us at www.ReaderService.com/consumerchoice or write to us at Reader Service Preference Service, P.O. Box 9062, Buffalo, NY 14240-9062. Include your complete name and address.

LIS15

SPECIAL EXCERPT FROM

Love Inspired
SUSPENSE

*After a hostage situation turns violent, Morgan Thorsby
is left injured—and sniper Brady Owens is left to carry a
new load of guilt, along with a determination to protect
Morgan from further harm…including a dangerously
possessive stalker who has made Morgan his target.*

Read on for a sneak peek of the action-packed adventure
HIGH-CALIBER HOLIDAY,
the latest story in the exciting miniseries
FIRST RESPONDERS.

Morgan came to a sudden stop. Brady couldn't react fast
enough to keep from bumping into her. He shot an arm
around her waist to stop her from taking a nosedive.
The glass fell from her hand, bouncing across the carpet
but not breaking. He expected her to push free, but she
clamped a hand over her mouth and pointed at the desk.

Brady followed the direction of her finger and found
three red roses and another picture lying on her pristine
desk.

"Not again." Brady's arm instinctively tightened around
her.

She tried to swivel out of his arms but he was holding
her too tight. He relaxed his grip just enough to allow her
to turn, but he couldn't make himself completely let go.

"Who could be doing this?" She lifted her stricken
gaze to his.

"Don't worry. We'll find out," he said, but he had no
reason at this point to believe they would.

"I'm so thankful for your help." A tremulous smile found her lips.

Hoping to put her at ease, he smiled back at her.

She suddenly seemed to notice he was holding her, and she pushed against his chest to free herself. The warmth of her touch sent his senses firing and his pulse racing. He didn't want to let go, but short of making a fool of himself, he had no other choice but to release her.

After dropping her bags on the desk, she reached for the picture.

"Don't touch it," he warned.

She snapped her hand back and bent closer to look. She suddenly gasped and lurched back. "He was in my room. Oh, no. No, no, no."

Knowing he wasn't going to like what he saw, Brady stepped closer. The picture was taken of Morgan from above. The shadow of the man taking the picture fell over her as she was peacefully sleeping in her bed. Superimposed on the bottom of the picture in bright red letters were the words *We'll soon be together forever, my love.*

Don't miss
HIGH-CALIBER HOLIDAY
by Susan Sleeman,
available November 2015 wherever
Love Inspired® Suspense books and ebooks are sold.

Turn your love of reading into
rewards you'll love with
Harlequin My Rewards

**Join for FREE today at
www.HarlequinMyRewards.com**

Earn **FREE BOOKS** of your choice.

Experience **EXCLUSIVE OFFERS** and contests.

Enjoy **BOOK RECOMMENDATIONS**
selected just for you.

PLUS! Sign up now
and get **500** points
right away!

Earn
FREE
REWARDS
HarlequinMyRewards.com
Join
Today!

MYR16R